# THE D

## Larry Stern

**SILVER MINK BOOKS**
PO Box CR25, Leeds LS7 3TN

New authors welcome

Printed and bound in Great Britain

Darker Side first published 1994
Copyright Larry Stern

*This is fiction - in real life, practice safe sex*

# THE REAL WENDY : A DEDICATION

'Wendy by Wire' is a fiction. As they say, 'there is no intended resemblance between the characters and events portrayed and anyone living or dead.' Well, maybe there is just a little ...

There was, as you may have guessed, a real Wendy, and it is largely because of her that these stories were written in the first place. I came into contact with her just as the narrator in the story encounters the fictional Wendy, through a computer bulletin board system. That's where fact and fiction diverge. Wendy's story is not that of the real Wendy. In fact Wendy and I never met although we did share what was, for me at least, an entertaining and enlightening correspondence.

What Wendy did, above all, was open my mind to the idea, and the acceptance of that notion, that love (or lust if you prefer) has a darker side. I learned from her and from later researches and experiences to which she opened me that there can be much intense sensual pleasure in acts of humiliation and chastisement, that the stroke of the whip can stimulate as effectively as a kiss or a caress.

So the stories that form this volume are drawn from that darker side which Wendy revealed to me by relating her own experiences and thus encouraging me to my own researches. It is only just, therefore, that the work be dedicated to its primary inspiration. Who knows, it may prompt her to contact the author once again ...

## WENDY BY WIRE

'Submissive girl seeking new master: Wendy'

My heart leaped into my mouth. Here was exactly what I had been looking for. That single line of text, the crisp white letters standing stark and clear against the phosphor green of my computer's screen, seemed to leap at me from among the handful of other one line adverts that surrounded it.

Since early that afternoon, when a friend who shares my interest in the exercise of male dominance and the enjoyment of female submission had told me about the 'Adult Bulletin Board', I had been itching to hook up to the telephone line and see for myself the delights it reputedly held on its memory banks. Now it seemed that my impatient wait was to be royally rewarded. Those few words were the stuff of which fantasies could and would be woven.

With trembling fingers, I typed the command to read the whole message and seconds later the distant computer printed on my screen:

'Hi, I'm Wendy. I am a submissive girl of 22. I have blue eyes, blonde hair and a 38-24-38 figure. My master used to say that that was just perfect for receiving punishment - a nice big bum I mean. Unfortunately my master and mistress have left the district. I am looking for someone to take me in hand. Can you help?'

I quickly typed in a response, introducing myself as a writer who specialised in stories dealing with female submissiveness and corporal punishment. I requested - no, I ordered - that Wendy should tell me more about herself and exactly what she had in mind. I closed by telling her to provide a detailed physical description of herself as if she were standing naked before a full length mirror. I closed the connection at that point and tried to keep myself occupied, despite my bubbling anticipation, until Wendy should have had sufficient time to send me her reply.

The next evening, with mounting excitement, I again sat at my keyboard and went through the process of establishing contact with the distant computer that held the bulletin board system. After a few seconds during which the two machines chattered in their electronic jargon, my video screen burst into life. Just as I had hoped, at the bottom of the screen were a few words indicating that a message awaited my attention. I typed in the necessary command and read:

'Thank you so very much for replying to my message. As you already know, my name is Wendy and I have a very submissive nature. I had a wonderful master and mistress - strict but also kind - who trained me and showed me the ways of obedience. Unfortunately they have had to leave the district and I could not accompany them. I am hoping to find someone who can become my master (or mistress) in their place. I thought that, at first, you might try to dominate me by exchanging messages through this bulletin board - I would do anything you say - and we could see how things progress.

'I work as a secretary cum PA to the Managing Director of an engineering firm up here in the north of England.

'You asked me to describe myself. I did as you directed and stood, naked, in front of my wardrobe mirror. This is what I saw.

'As you know already, I have blue eyes and blonde hair - well it's fair really not ash blonde or anything gorgeous like that. My hair is cut short and is shaped to outline my face. I have been told that I am quite pretty but I shall stick to the facts and not give opinions. I have a full-lipped mouth - sensual my master said - and a pert turned up nose.

'Progressing downwards, I have full, mature breasts as you would expect from my 38-24-38 measurements. Nevertheless my titties are taut and firm - the tips point perkily to the sky - which is one of the advantages of youth. They, my tits, are capped with brownish nipples set in deep aureolae. I am not suntanned, my master preferred pale flesh, so my tits are creamy peardrops. Continuing on, although I have a full figure which my master insisted I keep under control through rigorous exercise, my tummy is flat and taut except for a slight swell beneath my navel and down to my pubes.

'At the vee of my thighs, which are ripely fleshed ivory columns, stands my Mount of Venus which is covered with a thick thatch of fair hair which really does match the hair on my head. I suppose it now grows so thickly because my master would have me shaved down there from time to time. In fact once, as a punishment for some impudence, he made me shave off all my hair, even from my head. That may seem severe but, as I remember, I had been very naughty.

'Oh, I nearly forgot, I am about 5 feet 6 inches tall, so I am not exactly statuesque or willowy. My legs aren't dancer's legs either but they do look very shapely when I am wearing the five inch stiletto heels which were my master's particular favourite.

'Turning around now, you can see my bottom. Since I haven't been punished recently the flesh is unblemished and milky white. Of course, you already know that I have a big bottom; two hemispheres of firm flesh separated by the deep and mysterious furrow that conceals my tiny arse hole.

'I hope that I have described myself to your satisfaction. Respectfully and obediently: Wendy.'

I must admit that I did not hold out much hope of my being able to dominate this young woman as she wished through the medium of messages exchanged through computers. The subtle interworking of the dominant and submissive spirits, it seemed to me, required more immediate contact than would be possible through a telephone connection. How, I asked myself, could punishment be inflicted? One could hardly ask a victim to cane themselves - besides, the pleasure (and the benefit) resides in actually witnessing wood or leather striking yielding, cringing flesh and in enjoying the reddening of creamy bum-flesh and in hearing the squeals of pain. I was intrigued, however, to see to what conclusions our dialogue would progress and so I decided to persevere for the time being. I keyed in the following response,

'Your attempt at self description was barely adequate but will have to do until I acquaint you with my high standards. You represent yourself as a very attractive young woman. Your master and mistress must have derived much pleasure from your training. I would suppose that so obedient and well schooled a slave as you must be would have found a new master to serve with no difficulty.'

The next evening there was this response from Wendy:

'I do humbly apologise for not providing a response which meets your high standards. I hope you can forgive me.

'The trouble is that most men simply want to fuck me. While being used by a man for his sexual pleasure is an important part of being dominated, for me it is incomplete. The humiliation, the punishment, the submission to degradation are to me a very subtle form of foreplay without which the sex act is without point. I am afraid that most men cannot understand or take the time to meet my need.

'By the way, you have not mentioned how you would like me to dress when I am at your service. I have a very tight, black Basque which doesn't cover my breasts at all, merely supports them. I could wear that, black stockings of course, and black stiletto heeled shoes. Would this be acceptable?'

I replied at once:

'Your are forgetting your place. I will specify how you are to dress when I am ready. For now you will wear nothing, completely naked! Now for a punishment to remind you of the need to remember which of us is the master and who the slave. Fetch a hot water bottle and fill it with boiling water. Strip naked and sit on it at your keyboard. Now describe how it feels!'

The next evening Wendy's response awaited me:

'I have done as you ordered. Since I have never had to submit to such a punishment before (my master favoured spankings, birching and caning for the most part), I was filled with gloomy anticipation at having to undergo a very painful and unpleasant ordeal as I went about preparing my 'hot seat'. As you specified, I placed the bottle, filled with boiling water, on a hard chair I use when at my computer screen. I stripped quickly and gingerly lowered my bottom until the sensitive flesh was just brushing the hot water bottle. At once the heat stung my poor fesses and I had to fight hard against my first inclination which was to withdraw and disobey you.

'I persevered, however, and gradually increased the contact, lowering my bottom until I was seated firmly on the hot surface. The pain was intense and I screwed my eyes tight shut against it and grasped the arms of the chair to force myself to remain seated. I wriggled and squirmed which, if anything, intensified the hurt which was like having the skin peeled from my bottom, strip by strip.

'Quite quickly, though, the water cooled off and my bottom became used to the heat. I got up and looked at my rear end in a mirror. My poor bum is glowing bright red just like a boiled lobster and it is throbbing awfully. Now I wish I had a nice kind master or mistress with me to comfort me a little.'

As I read these words I was suddenly struck by how I might capitalise on this, to me, rather unsatisfactory experience. Wendy had obviously enjoyed her punishment but to me it lacked the satisfying edge of actually viewing the event, of seeing the anguish on her face and of giving a few extra slaps to her tenderised buttocks for good measure. Quickly I typed this message:

'Now we will play Arabian Nights. You must tell me the details of your life as a slave, being candid and leaving nothing out. If I am pleased you will escape punishment. If not you will submit as I specify. First tell me how you met your master and mistress and fell under their domination.'

For two evenings after that there was no message from Wendy. I was beginning to think that she had lost interest and that I would hear no more from her. On the third evening, however, there was the following message waiting for me:

'I apologise most humbly for the delay in answering you. I wanted to make sure that you would be pleased with the candour and fullness of my response and so I took a lot of time and trouble over it. Anyway, here goes.

'I used to live in quite a small village in the country but when I was eighteen I came to this city and found a job as a junior secretary. I got a flat, living on my own rather than share, and set about enjoying the bright lights and the social scene. I had a few boyfriends but nothing serious or long-term. I enjoyed my job in a big, friendly office. Everything was fine.

'Yes, everything was fine except that I was a complete innocent when it came to managing money. My salary was hardly enough to keep up the rent on my flat and to live on. Maybe I should have found someone to share but it just didn't occur to me. Anyway, after living at home with a brother and two sisters I valued my privacy. In the end I resorted to credit cards to make ends meet, hardly thinking that these debts and the interest on them would all have to be paid one day.'

'My various debts soon mounted to unmanageable proportions. I was alone in this city apart from a few superficial friendships I had made and so I had no-one to turn to for advice. In the end I just paid the most pressing creditor with whatever money I had and let the rest continue to mount up. That is how the rent on my flat came to be three months in arrears.

'I had been paying my rent to the landlord's agent, a firm of solicitors. Their letters when I failed to pay the first and second months rent were politely formal and so I felt that I could safely ignore them. When I missed the third month no letter came. Instead, one Saturday afternoon, my landlord turned up in person.

'That was the first time that I met the man who was soon to become my master and I his most willing slave. Eric, though I never used his name, was a tall, very well built man in vigorous middle-age. He had a full head of thick, iron gray hair which was swept back from his forehead, and the most piercing steel blue eyes. He was certainly handsome in a refined and very English way, something after the manner of Stewart Granger.

'He introduced himself and asked if he might come in. I was in no position to refuse!

'Once in the living room Eric came straight to the point. When could he expect payment of what I owed and what had been the difficulty in the last few months? Confronted with one of my creditors in the flesh, there was nothing for it but to tell the truth. The whole sorry story came out and I ended up in floods of tears. Eric put a comforting arm about my shoulders and drew me to him, letting me bury my face in his broad chest.

'He let me sob away for a little while and I dampened the front of his shirt with my tears. Then, still holding me to him, he said gently, "Look here, my dear, I think that you are in urgent need of help. I believe that my wife and I can do something for you but you will need to put yourself entirely in our hands. Now if I can use the telephone, I'll call home to check that my good lady is in agreement."

'Unable to speak through my sobs, I indicated the whereabouts of the telephone in the hall and Eric left me alone while he made his call. I was feeling reassured already and began to pull myself together. Here was someone at last who would take over and solve my problems, just like my father would have. I was sure that I could rely on this great, solid man who seemed so gentle and caring.

'Eric soon returned and told me that his wife was in full agreement with his proposal which he then went on to explain. I was to give up the flat which was patently too expensive for my current means and I should go to live with Eric and his wife, who was called Alice. I was to give Eric my credit cards and he would take care of all of my outstanding bills which amounted to some three thousand pounds. Thereafter I would give my wages to Eric and Alice who would manage the money until, as I supposed, I was considered capable of sorting out my own affairs.

'So far this seemed to be a heaven sent solution to my overwhelming problems. Eric went on to explain that while I stayed in his home I should be expected to

13

be obedient to his and Alice's wishes as far as conduct, timekeeping, mealtimes and so forth were concerned and that any infractions would be punished. Was I willing to submit to those punishments? Without hesitation, still feeling the warm glow that the offer of salvation had induced, I agreed that I was willing to accept the conditions he stated.

'Still Eric continued to set out further conditions. I would be expected to help Alice in the house and act as a sort of companion. In short I was to place myself wholly in their hands and submit myself to their wishes. Was I still in agreement?

'It seemed to me that I had very little choice. Anyway, the conditions as Eric had explained them did not seem too onerous when compared to the fix I had found myself in. So I agreed quite readily and without much reflection on the possible consequences.

'Eric told me to get together a few overnight things so that we could leave straightaway, assuring me that we would come back for the rest of my clothes the next day. I did as he asked and was soon closing the door of the flat behind me for the last time. We descended to the street and climbed into Eric's waiting car and soon after had reached the tree lined streets and open grassy spaces of the city's outer suburbs.

'Eric and Alice lived in just such a suburban avenue, occupying a large, detached house which was set back from the street and was well separated from its neighbours by a neatly kept garden. It was obvious that here everybody minded their own business and that neighbours rarely encountered one another. Darkness was drawing on as Eric helped me from the car and escorted me through the front door.

'He lead me straight through the spacious hall and up the wide staircase to the upper floor of the house and ushered me into a bedroom at the end of the landing. My room, for such it was to be for the next four years, was not spacious but neither was it a cramped boxroom. It had been newly decorated, almost as if against my imminent arrival, and was neatly furnished with bed, dressing table and a small writing desk. On the narrow single bed, which was arranged along one wall, was a neat pile of clothes.

'Eric put down my case and gestured towards the folded garments, "You see that my good lady has laid out a few things for you. I'm sure you will understand that it will please her no end if you wear them this evening. Just slip them on and come down to the dining room and then we can all get acquainted."

'There was no opportunity to argue the point as Eric slipped away, closing the door behind him. Anyway, I thought, still high on the feeling of relief at escaping from my debts, it would be no hardship to wear the clothes my benefactors had provided. Quickly then, I stripped off the worn jeans and sweater I had been wearing when Eric had first appeared on my doorstep and picked up the garments from the pile in the middle of my bed.

'On closer examination it seemed that my hosts expected me to wear a sort of school uniform. It was all there - grey pleated skirt that reached to just below the knee, plain white blouse which was crisply starched, white ankle socks, even white cotton knickers. All of it, strangely enough, was just my size, which as you probably realise now is not exactly schoolgirlish. I shrugged my shoulders, chasing any lingering doubts from my mind and got dressed.

'I was just about ready and was passing a comb through my hair when I chanced to glance around the room. For the first time I took real note of my surroundings. This room reminded me so strongly of my own bedroom at home with my parents. Then it dawned on me. This was indeed a schoolgirl's room even down to the writing desk for homework. Some grown up and departed daughter's I assumed, and without a further thought I set off downstairs to meet my two benefactors.

'In the hall a call from one of the rooms guided me to the dining room and for the first time I met my new mistress. She, like Eric, was in middle-age but a well-preserved middle-age. Alice was slim and shapely with twinkling brown eyes and short chestnut hair which was attractively flecked with grey. She held out a soft and well-manicured hand to me and invited me to join them at table.

'So the three of us sat down to what was to all appearance a normal family tea. There were dainty sandwiches, a currant cake and Alice poured tea -Milk or lemon, my dear? - from a silver teapot.

'We chatted, of course. Eric and Alice told me some of their background, especially about their own two children who were now grown up and well established in the USA. I had been right in my surmise that the room assigned to me had been their own daughter's when she was at home. For my part, I chatted on about my own home, my family, my job and carefully avoided all mention of the embarrassing events that had brought me here as a beneficiary of Eric and Alice's hospitality.

'Eventually the meal was finished and the superficial chatter was at an end. Alice turned to me with a somewhat sterner expression on her face, "Now Wendy, I think it is time that we got to the subject that has really brought us all together. I mean your culpable foolishness and our desire to help you overcome it and its consequences. Let us go into the living room where we can be more comfortable."

'Not at all wishing to talk again of my money troubles and particularly my indebtedness to her and her husband, my heart sank. Nevertheless, I followed the couple into the brightly lit living room. Alice seated herself at one end of a long couch while Eric took up his station at the other end.'

'"I think it will be most appropriate if you kneel there," Alice instructed as she pointed to a small kneeling stool that had been placed in the middle of the room. I was dumbstruck and hesitated, completely unsure of what was happening and how I should react.

'Alice's firm tones soon showed me how I must act. "I understood from Eric that you had agreed to place yourself in our hands and to obey us in everything that we considered appropriate to your future education and well-being. That was the undertaking, was it not Eric?" Eric nodded agreement. "Then kneel or leave - the choice is still yours."

'How could I leave? Leave with my debts still around my neck? Leave with only my home in the country to go back to? Kneeling before my benefactors as a humiliated supplicant didn't seem much after all. I got down on my knees and faced them.

'"Now," Alice continued, "let us be clear. We have agreed to manage your debts and your future finances, to give you a home here with us, to repair some of the deficiencies in your education that an upbringing lacking strict discipline (which is a deplorable modern fashion) has left. You agree to make yourself serviceable to us as we choose and to submit to the rules and discipline that we impose. Is that clear and acceptable to you?"

'I nodded my agreement but Alice prompted me until I said clearly, "Yes, I understand and accept."

'"Good, we are making progress at last," Alice continued with just the trace of a smile. "I am sure you have heard the saying 'Confession is good for the soul'. Eric and I both agree most strongly that that is so. Now then, for the good of your soul, let us hear you confess and acknowledge the shortcomings which have brought you here."

'There was nothing for it but to tell over again the recklessness, the stupidity and the selfishness which had saddled me with a mountain of debt. I blushed hotly and sometimes stammered, at times my throat thickened and tears welled up. I had thought myself a young woman of eighteen but here I was, proven on my own admission, nothing but a silly child. At last, mortified, I ended the litany of my sins.

'"Well done! I am sure that you feel much better already," Alice remarked. And, strangely, I did feel a certain relief, a certain lightness.

"'I must also tell you now, Wendy, that another old saying we believe to be true is, 'Spare the rod and spoil the child.' We were certainly not slow to punish our own children and we intend to treat you just as strictly. I'm sure you will agree that the tale you have told us certainly merits a punishment."

'How could I do anything but agree? In fact at this point, with the humiliation of confession still fresh, I did agree. I had never been punished as a child, maybe it would do me good.

"'Excellent. I am glad to find you so tractable," Alice positively beamed. "Tonight I think it will be enough if Eric just spanks your bottom. We shall see what else might be needed later on. Stand up and raise your skirt."

'I hesitated very slightly but the stern look was already starting to cloud Alice's normally benign features. I jumped to my feet and hiked my skirt above my waist. I was acutely conscious of my large, well fleshed bottom straining at the tight cotton underpants and of Eric's gaze savouring every curve and dimple of my lower anatomy.

"'Pants off, if you please!" and I slipped the garment over my posterior and down my legs. Eric had brought a straight backed chair and sitting upon it he indicated wordlessly that I should drape myself over his lap. I did as I was told with no protest. Deftly he flipped my skirt up to my waist to bare my rump for the punishment prescribed.

'I think I have already shown that Eric was a powerful and vigorous man. When his large hand connected with my poor bottom I found out just how powerful. A steady rain of stinging blows punished my quivering nates until my bum was glowing hotly like a beacon fire. Eric made sure that no inch of my juddering flesh was left unvisited and his sure and stinging touch covered me from waist to thigh. I yelped with pain and surprise and with no little indignity as for some fifteen minutes my bottom felt the weight of his hand.

'Judging that I had had enough, at least for my first time, Eric left off spanking me and let me get to my feet. My bum glowed hotly and ached awfully but beneath it all there was a delicious bitter-sweet tingling. And, to my surprise, I did feel a lot better about myself. Somehow the pain and the indignity had, in my mind, secured for me a little forgiveness.

'Then I had to stand awhile with my skirts bunched at the waist while Alice and Eric admired his handiwork. Finally Alice remarked that it was well past my bedtime and I was packed off to my room after first having to thank Eric for so kindly spanking my bum.

'Upstairs I made my preparations for bed and had just slipped between the sheets, feeling the delicious coolness on my ever throbbing nates when the door opened and in walked my two benefactors. Both of them, with a smile, kissed me on the cheek and Alice tucked me in just as if I were a child. Then without a further word they left, turning out the light and leaving me to sleep. End of message.'

Quite naturally I was very pleased with Wendy's narrative, nevertheless some punishment was in order to chastise her for keeping me waiting for her response to my order and, of course, because she would expect it. I thought long and hard but could come up with nothing that would give us both pleasure since every possibility I canvassed lacked that vital component - my own direct and tangible participation. At last I decided to settle for a vicarious pleasure. I sat at the keyboard and typed:

'Your story was acceptable - just. Your tardiness in complying with my instruction was not and you must suffer for it.

'You said that your old master was keen for you to exercise regularly. I suspect that since you are now without supervision and are probably quite lazy, you now neglect this necessary part of your routine. So for your punishment you will take a little exercise. Tonight I want you to do fifty press-ups followed by fifty sit-ups. Do them properly mind. No fudging. Arms fully stretched and so on. You must be naked when you do this, nevertheless I expect you will work up quite a sweat. So afterwards, into the shower, cold naturally, and stay there for a full fifteen minutes.

'When you recover, I want to know some more about your life with Eric and Alice. Sex must have entered the relationship. Tell me how and do not shirk the detail.'

The next evening there was this reply from Wendy:

'Phew, my muscles are still aching from all that exercise, especially my poor tummy. And I have only just stopped shivering. I almost turned blue under that shower. Still, I would probably have got much worse from you if you had been here! Anyway, you don't like to be kept waiting so here is some more of my story.

'After that first evening my new found master and mistress gradually introduced me to my new life of service and obedience. Yet, so subtle was this introduction, that I found myself readily embracing each new imposition, submitting to each new form of punishment or restriction and suddenly found myself enjoying the whole process. I must stress that I was never made a slave but rather was treated as a somewhat wayward and silly daughter in a strictly regulated, even Victorian, household. It has to be said that in those early stages I actually derived great comfort from having the two of them regulate my life to such an extent. After all I had got into such trouble on my own.

'The next morning Alice visited my flat and reviewed my wardrobe, most of which she found to be totally unsuitable. On the Monday, therefore, I accompanied her to buy new, more suitable clothing of her choosing. Many of the new items were quite conservative and always of the best quality. Others were more exotic, or should I say erotic - my black Basque for example. So it was that I was always dressed in a fashion of my master and mistress' choosing, never of my own. Later, in fact, there would be times when I was not allowed clothing at all. It was a strange sensation, at first, to sit down to dinner stark naked but flanked by two fully clothed companions.

'It was made clear from the start that I should continue to work at my job but that all my earnings should pass into the control of my benefactors. Each morning Eric would drive me to work and each evening, prompt at five o' clock, would come again to collect me. When I was not working I would be set to help Alice in the house which ultimately meant that I became cook, cleaner and gardener under my mistress' direction as well as rendering both Eric and her certain more personal services.

'Gradually both of them also contrived to introduce me to more and more rigorous and varied forms of corporal punishment. They were careful never to push me beyond the bounds of reason and to demonstrate that the punishment prescribed was for my own good. Thus, by progressive steps, I was introduced to the tawse, the birch and the riding crop and found to my amazement a true release and enjoyment in my submission. But now you wish to hear of how my master and mistress used me sexually ...

'A few weeks had passed since I had first come to live with Eric and Alice. Receiving my due dose of punishment every so often had quite become a way of life and now I had been subjected to spankings, canings and the tawse. On this particular evening Eric had been attending to my bottom with the supple leather of a fine example of the Scottish instrument of correction. I was on my knees with my head cushioned on my arms on the seat of the sofa while my bare bottom stuck up in the air, blushing hotly and stinging terrifically. I was dressed in my 'school uniform' again, with the full pleated skirt bunched up about my waist and the white panties lying discarded on the floor.

'Eric tossed the tawse onto the sofa and, ordering me to stay where I was, disappeared briefly from the room. On his return he told me to stand and I saw that he had taken off his clothes, replacing them with a terrycloth robe that reached nearly to his bare feet. I surmised, quite correctly, that beneath the robe he was stark naked.

23

'He sat in an armchair and beckoned me to sit on his lap. I certainly understood what was about to happen and gladly settled myself on his legs with the rough towelling of the robe chafing my glowing flesh. For some time now I had noticed how Eric's manhood would stiffen and try to burrow at my navel as I lay across his lap while his large hands slapped heartily at my quivering buttocks. I was no innocent and had slept with a few boys. Now I found increasingly that my submissive position and the attention so regularly paid to my posteriors made me - well, randy, is the only word. I wriggled my bottom and brushed my thigh against Eric's groin, assuring myself that his penis had again attained a pleasing state of tumescence.

'"Now, my dear, just sit perfectly still and do as I tell you," Eric murmured as his fingers deftly unfastened the buttons of my blouse. Soon the crisp cotton was pushed from my shoulders and down over my arms, trapping them at my sides. Reaching behind me, Eric loosed the catch of my bra with one hand and dragged it forward and down to both bare my breasts and further secure my arms. At the sight of my ripe, ivory flesh and the flaccid nipples the hard male member against my thigh gave a satisfying twitch.

'Gently at first but then with increasing firmness, Eric cupped a yielding mound of flesh in each large hand and massaged my boobs. The massage became a squeeze, became a moulding, a pulling and resolved again to firm massaging. My breasts began to swell with excitement and the sleepy nipple buds awoke to grind into the palms of his hand.

'Eric took one ripe fruit on the palm of his hand and bending his head fed warm flesh between his lips. Teeth ground on the suave flesh and worried gobbets of ripeness. His tongue rasped over a nipple which was bullet hard by now. He sucked, drawing it into his mouth to trap it between tongue and palate. Ripples of pleasure flowed through me and I groaned or rather purred in the back of my throat. Leaving that breast he lavished a similar attention on the other, smearing my flesh wetly with his saliva.

'His hands were busy now releasing me from blouse and bra, tossing them carelessly to the floor.

'"Hands on your head. Stick out you tits," he whispered and I obeyed. Then hands, lips, teeth and tongue were busy over my bared flesh. His tongue drew trails of wetness over my armpits; lips and teeth worried my neck as his hands caressed the soft flesh of my belly. Again and again, though, he returned to my titties, moulding and squeezing, kneading, licking and sucking as sensations of the purest sexual electricity flowed to my core.

'I felt his practised fingers release the waistband of my skirt and a gesture of his hand invited me to raise my bottom. I did so and the grey cotton was drawn down my legs to leave me naked but for my virginally white ankle socks. Firm hands parted my legs and stroked along the plump damp flesh of the inner thigh drawing ever closer to my womanhood. I could feel myself soaking wet, the juices of my overheated quim bathing the swollen lips of my sex.

'Still nibbling and sucking at my tit, Eric now caressed my sex. Gently his fingers parted my nether lips and paddled in my wetness. Two then three fingers frigged into my sopping cunt, parting the lips, brushing the walls of muscle, thrilling my loins. Eric left off his assault on my titties and stared penetratingly into my eyes as his fingers plunged in and out of my sex. Then he found the stiff nodule of my clitoris and rubbed the tiny bundle of delights with his thumb as his fingers rasped inside me.

'Wave after wave of pure electric pleasure burst over me. I felt as if my head would explode. I shut my eyes, screamed, moaned, bit my lip and with a shudder that rippled through my frame, I came.

'When I regained a grip on my senses, eyes still swimming from the sheer intensity of my release, I became aware of an insistent hardness pushing against my thigh. Eric's manhood, hugely, angrily erect, had escaped from the folds of his robe and was demanding my attention.

'"On your knees, my dear, and attend to our friend here," came Eric's soft voiced but firm command.

'Obediently I slipped to my knees between my master's outstretched legs. Eric parted the terry-cloth robe to show that he was indeed naked underneath. His phallus reared up from the forest of dark pubic curls at his groin; a thick, rigid pole. Tentatively, I reached out and grasped it at the root as I passed my other hand beneath the velvet sac of his scrotum feeling the delicate eggs that nestled within. I knew that I wanted to do homage to this powerful throbbing beast with my mouth but here I was a clumsy innocent. I had never before received a man in my mouth.

'As it was, I had but to follow Eric's instructions as he whispered urgently his requirements of me. First I licked over the fat, juicy titbit, coating it from tip to base with my saliva until it gleamed dully in the lamplight. I played my tongue over the smooth skin of his scrotum, teasing the eggs within, drawing the purse between my lips. Then I must take him into my mouth - first the dome, fat and purple like a Victoria plum, then lips nibbling the ridge of the glans, the stem followed. I forced my jaws apart to take him all inside, every millimetre of throbbing flesh, until my mouth was crammed full of him.

'Maniacally I began to suck and lick at the living, pulsing, twitching beast. Raising and lowering my head I allowed the beast to fuck my mouth, pumping saliva from the back of my throat, coating him richly, easing his passage. Meanwhile my hands played over his taut thighs, over his belly and sought his buttocks as if to lift him to my mouth.

'Very soon, amid my frenzy as I tried to ingest the beast, to force his huge, thick penis down my throat, I felt him throb and realised suddenly that Eric was about to spend, pumping his rich, hot cream into my mouth. I panicked and released him just as his first spurt of delicious creamy goo erupted from him to splash squarely over my face. I could do nothing then but hold on to the jerking weapon as eruption followed eruption spraying semen over my tits, shoulders, arms and finally dribbling in my hand as the tumescence wilted.

'I was covered in the delicious effusion and just knelt there not knowing what was expected of me. Eric spoke gently, "You are in a real mess - spunk all over you.

Next time you must try to swallow a little. Off to the bathroom with you and wash yourself. Then come straight back here."

'I padded off to the bathroom and cleaned myself up just as I had been told and hurried back to the living room. Eric stood in the middle of the room, quite naked and once again fully erect.

'My master directed me to get up on the sofa and to kneel on all fours with my bottom presented to him. He took up his position behind me and nestled his rock hard erection between my bum cheeks, grinding his belly against my meaty posteriors while his hands roved over my body, luxuriating in my well fleshed frame. Then parting the lips of my sex he placed the head of his penis at the porch of my womanhood and drew me backwards onto his thick staff to embed himself in my drooling sex. As his thickness cleaved my flesh and my cunny muscles clasped him a thrill of orgasm churned through me.

'He fucked me then - slowly at first but with increasing vigour, bouncing my tits and rippling my flesh. Wave after wave of pleasure broke over me as the thick, solid rod reamed in and out of my well pleasured pussy. Suddenly Eric ceased his thrusting and clamped me to himself, grasping my hips as his spend jetted from him to fill me to overflowing.

'He withdrew from me and as my vision cleared from the clouds of pleasure, I saw Alice standing in the doorway, smiling broadly.

'"That was quite delightful, my dear. But now I think it is time for bed." And so it was.

'A couple of days later - it was a Sunday as I remember - it was Alice's turn to initiate me into the pleasures of Sapphic love.

'Among the various duties that now fell to me was the job of assisting my mistress at her morning toilette each Saturday and Sunday morning. This was a fairly lengthy process during which Alice took every opportunity to pamper herself, luxuriating in hot, foaming baths, using creams and unguents on her skin which was still unblemished and smooth as silk and carefully applying perfumes and cosmetics. I helped with all these tasks, fetching and carrying and becoming quite accomplished as a lady's maid.

'On this particular Sunday my mistress had already bathed and I had helped her to apply the unguents and perfumes to her supple flesh. She lay back, absolutely naked, in a plumply cushioned cane chair and eyed me knowingly.

'"You and Eric seemed to have enjoyed yourselves the other night," she began in a soft drawl, her voice charged with lust. She was, of course, stating the obvious. Eric had rogered me to heaven and had himself been well pleasured in the process. "Now, my dear, it is our turn. On your knees and use your mouth here," and she indicated her sex which already pouted wetly amidst her pubic thatch.

'I knelt and approached my face to Alice's sex, the soft skin of her inner thighs brushing my cheeks. The musky scent of her desire mingled with her perfume to produce a heady and exciting odour. My blood raced and I bent eagerly to taste this new experience.

29

'Tentatively I drew my tongue, wet and willing, over the swollen labiae. Alice purred her approval and urged me on, husking explicit instructions. With just my tongue, I probed her nether lips which parted easily to let me taste the rich flavour of her juices. I persevered and soon my tongue, straining from its root, was embedded in the hot, treacly warmth while my lips pressed firmly against her labiae. I sucked hard and worked my tongue in the hot, velvety cavern for all I was worth. Alice encouraged me with groans of lust, grasping my head and grinding my face against the mouth of her sex.

'After some little while I managed to draw back a little, my mouth and chin now ringed with my mistress' sticky discharge. I used my hands to part her sex lips, forming Alice's womanhood into a gaping gash. There at the top of this canyon of flesh I glimpsed, stiffly erect and surprisingly large, the sensitive bud of her clitoris. With slow and gentle motions, starting at the lower extremity close to her anus and progressing upwards to finish at her clitty I lapped sensuously at her sex. My head bobbed slowly up and down and my tongue licked the juices from her before wrapping itself, briefly, around the sensitive knot of nerve endings.

'Alice's breath came in deep pants and she was groaning continuously as the sweet sensations rippled though her. Instinctively I knew that now I must work to bring her to her ultimate climax. I concentrated my tongue on her clitoris, increasing the pace of my lapping, pressing my tongue tip hard against the fat bud. It had the desired effect. Alice's thighs clamped me to her and she screamed deliriously as her orgasm swept over her.

'Releasing me, she lay back panting and with a broad smile on her lips. "Delicious, my sweet, you have a natural ability. Now off with your clothes and lie down on the bed."

'I was only wearing a thin cotton nightdress which I quickly pulled up over my head and in glorious anticipation climbed baby naked onto the double bed that Alice usually shared with my master.

'Alice joined me in a trice, embracing me, naked flesh on warm, naked flesh. Our bodies moulded together, breasts flattened against breasts, nipples crushing nipples, bellies grinding, legs entwined. Alice kissed me, open mouthed, our tongues sucking wetly as she tasted her own sex taste. Our flesh mingled and her weight bore down on me. Taking her time, she tasted my flesh, dragging lips and tongue and teeth over shoulders, breasts and belly until at last she reached my Mount. Her hand kneaded the pudenda, fingers teased the tangle of pubic hair.

'Automatically I parted my thighs. I glimpsed her eyes as she raised her head. They were glassy, glazed with desire. Then her face was pressed hard against my cunt, tongue lapping, lips sucking. Alice now performed the same office for me as I had for her - using her mouth to raise me to ever higher plateaux of pleasure until at last the ultimate tidal wave of orgasm should wash over me.

'I had just reached the cusp of pleasure, about to dive into that whirlpool of the senses when at the edge of my vision I became aware that Eric was with us. He stood, stark naked, beside the bed. He was heavily erect and idly stroked his straining tool. Then I was coming and my whole being focused on the pleasure that was spreading from my loins. With my eyes tightly shut I squealed with blissful release as my climax came.

'When I regained my senses I again became aware of Eric standing beside the bed, still cradling the thick pole of his manhood in his palm.

'"Come, Wendy, I believe that Eric wishes to join us." And with this remark, Alice positioned herself on all fours to present her rear end to her husband. I followed her example and knelt beside her to offer my master a choice of two willing and ready cunts.

'Eric was equal to the task and, grasping my hips firmly, he slipped his erect member easily into my well lubricated channel. Before me there was a mirror doored wardrobe which afforded me an excellent view as my master worked at me. As he steadily rammed his erection back and forth inside me, Eric passed a hand around me to fondle the fecund flesh of my belly and, creeping lower, to massage the sensitive bud of my clitoris. Little wavelets of pleasure coursed through me as my cunny muscles clasped his weapon and his fingers stimulated me. I whimpered tiny groans of happiness.

'When he judged that I had enjoyed sufficient of this play, Eric slipped from me and mounted Alice in her turn to perform a similar ministration upon her with like effect. Turn and turn about he worked on us, seemingly capable of holding himself in check forever while pleasuring us continuously.

'My master made sure that both of us had enjoyed at least one thoroughly shattering climax apiece as he burrowed his massy rod into our respective chasms. My head was swimming with lust and my thighs were starting to tremble. Suddenly, with his penis still rammed to the hilt in my steaming quim, Eric let go my clitty and began to probe with his love juice soaked forefinger at the tight ring of my anus. I was perfectly relaxed and it took but little effort on his part to wriggle his digit fully into my bumhole. I took it all in my stride and pushed back against his hand as I enjoyed the strange new sensations in my back passage.

'Eric murmured something to Alice and she instantly left my side. My master unplugged his still iron rigid member from my cunt and I watched in the mirror as Alice smeared cream from the pot she had fetched over the tip of the throbbing beast. Realisation dawned. Eric meant to fuck me in the arse. I was on such a 'high', so excited by the lustful events that had already taken place that I was only too willing to experience this new violation and so I wriggled my bottom eagerly as his forefinger continued to skewer me.

'With a distinct 'plop' Eric withdrew his finger and at once introduced the tip of his weapon at the porch of my fundament. He grasped my hips firmly and began to penetrate my arsehole with a single steady and irresistible thrust. There was some pain as the tightly constricted ring of my bum hole stretched to receive him but following the pain, new and delightful sensations washed over me. I was very tight and my anus squeezed Eric's erection as he worked in my fundament so that it needed just a few short strokes before a twitching in the hot flesh rod clasped in my anal channel signalled the onset of his climax. Hot gushes of creamy goo spilled from him to fill my bumhole and, as he withdrew, the creamy tribute spurted over my bumcheeks and trickled over my thighs.

'So that is how I was first accustomed to be used by my master and mistress. From then on they used me often and at will. I hope my story has pleased you but, of course, I will accept any punishment you may consider necessary to make up for my shortcomings.'

I could hardly have found her account less than fascinating and I was anxious to have yet more details of her life with the couple who had first shown her the pleasure to be derived from submission and obedience. I was at a loss, however, to think of a suitable punishment for her although it was obvious that she expected to receive one. Maybe, I argued with myself, in this case no punishment would be the best punishment since she seemed so eager to suffer. I sat at the keyboard and typed:

'I will not punish you - yet! You mentioned that your master and mistress used the birch on you. Describe how you were introduced to this punishment and let the recollection of the birch twigs biting and bruising your flesh prepare you for punishments to come.'

I was forced, now, to wait three or four days before another message from Wendy awaited me. In that time I wondered if she too was beginning to find domination without direct contact as unsatisfying as I. Her message began:

'I am sorry to take so long to respond. I do hope that I have not provoked your anger too greatly. Anyway, here is the story of my first birching. I hope it pleases you.

'My master and mistress very quickly came to realise that my formal education had been sorely neglected. I had left school with a bare minimum of qualifications, barely sufficient to secure my very junior office job. In their own words, Eric and Alice thought that a girl as attractive and basically intelligent as they considered myself, warranted the opportunity to develop her talents. It would be good for me and also fit me better to serve them.

'So, in the little time that remained after working at my office job, cooking, cleaning and helping Alice, suffering punishment and yielding to Alice and Eric's carnal appetites, I was to follow a quite taxing programme of formal education. I was to learn to play the piano, study French and improve my English. As it turned out, Alice had been a teacher (hence the interest in discipline, I suppose) and could quite easily tutor me in all of these subjects.

'Quite naturally, with all the other calls on my time and my own disinclination to study, I did not give myself to my books as wholeheartedly and zealously as my master and mistress might have wished. Practice was not as assiduously done as it might have been, assignments were late and did not reach the expected standard. The ultimate outcome of all this, unsurprisingly, was that I was punished. Usually this would simply consist of spankings or a taste of the tawse with me sprawled over Eric or Alice's lap, offering them free access to my bare bum. On those occasions when I had been especially naughty, however, something special - specially painful and specially humiliating - was called for.

'The first birching I received was all because of irregular French verbs. I had already made one attempt at learning the wretched things but when Alice tested me my mind was a complete blank. My mistress, with great forbearance, gave me another week to try to cram the declension lists into my skull. Then, on a Saturday evening, when other girls of my age would be getting ready to go out with or in search of a boyfriend, I stood before my inquisitor dressed in the outfit of a somewhat overgrown schoolgirl.

'It wasn't surprising that I made a similar poor showing to that of the week before. Lack of time and lack of inclination had meant that I had not even opened the text book since my last encounter with my mistress. Alice treated me to a withering look over the top of her glasses which made me feel even more like a naughty schoolgirl than ever. My cheeks were bright crimson as, with downcast eyes, I admitted that I had been lazy, idle and inattentive to my mistress' wishes.

'"I think that such laziness and disobedience calls for a fitting punishment, something out of the ordinary," Alice opined and turned to Eric who, as always, silently occupied a seat at his wife's side as I underwent examination of my academic progress. "What do you think, Eric?"

'"Oh, quite so, my dear," Eric concurred. "You know, I believe I have just the thing. You recall that I have been preparing some new birch rods - they are in the brine tank curing right now. How do you think a birching might suit our purpose?"

'I was well used to the harsh kiss of leather and the spanking hand on my poor backside by now but the

36

mention of birching still sent a shiver down my spine. I had read all about this form of punishment in some of the more prurient Sunday newspapers and knew roughly what to expect.

'"Just the thing, Eric. And tomorrow morning would be just the time."

'So it was settled and I passed a sleepless night in anticipation of the severe beating that my poor bottom would have to sustain on the morrow.

'Early next morning, straight after breakfast, Alice and Eric lead me, with my stomach churning, to the place of execution. Attached to the house was a double garage, a side door from the kitchen gave access to this outbuilding without the need to actually go outside of the house. As they led me into the garage Eric explained, quite casually, that a lot of room was required when swinging a four foot birch so the garage would be the perfect place. This did nothing to relieve my feelings of apprehension - the thought of a four foot bundle of birch twigs smashing onto my unprotected bum simply filled me with dismay.

'Inside, the garage was well heated and brilliantly lit by several neon tubes suspended overhead. A sturdy bench or table which was just about waist height was placed in the middle of the available area and was obviously there to support me as I underwent punishment.

'"Now, Wendy, we shall have you naked for your chastisement. Off with your clothes and let us hear you confess to the crimes which have brought you here."

'For the occasion I had dressed in a simple summer frock, belted at the waist and reaching loosely to just above my knees. I hadn't bothered with stockings or pants, guessing that I wouldn't be wearing much for very long. Quickly then, quite anxious to get it all over with, I took off the belt and slipped the dress over my head. I fumbled a little with the catch of my bra in my haste, then it was undone and my heavy breasts were tumbling free. I stood there quite naked except for my black court high-heeled shoes.

"'I am very sorry for my laziness," I began my formal confession, hands clasped behind me and head bowed in the posture of contrition I had been taught. Oddly, although I was quite used to being unclothed in the presence of my master and mistress, these new circumstances made me blush hotly with embarrassment. I was now doubly conscious of both of them gazing avidly at my naked body, my flaring hips, fecund belly and punishable arse.

"'I humbly beg you to give me the punishment I so richly deserve." I finished my confession in the time honoured fashion and stood waiting for my master and mistress to command me. Eric produced the birch he intended to use on me and held out the mass of twigs for me to inspect and again I shuddered at being confronted by the tangible evidence of the torment to come. Then, having been made to have a good look at the birch, Alice bent me over the punishment bench, making sure as she did so that my upper body was well flattened against the wooden top and that my bottom was well pushed out to receive the strokes to come. She spread my legs and with strong cords secured my wrists and ankles so that I was unable to flinch or avoid the rain of blows which would descend imminently.

'I held my breath as I felt the rough twigs cares the distended hemispheres of my buttocks, conscious of the large and fleshy target they presented. There was a distant 'swish' as the birch cleaved the air and then searing pain as the bundle of twigs smashed against my bum. I howled long and loud, straining against my bonds as the flood of hurt suffused my quivering flesh.

'Alice intoned the count of strokes as Eric applied the birch to my fesses, covering me from waist to thigh. The buds bit at my tender flesh, tearing the skin as the pain intensified with each slash of wood over burning flesh. I closed my eyes and tears coursed unchecked down my cheeks. I clasped the edge of the table, whitening the knuckles of my hand. I wriggled my poor tortured bum as the birch bit my fesses again and again with deliberate precision.

'"Fifteen ... That I think is sufficient, Eric."

'I sighed with relief on hearing those words. My poor bottom was burning and all the backs of my thighs from just above the knee glowed hotly. Despite the pain, however, the heat had also entered my pussy and I felt overwhelmingly randy.

'Eric tossed aside the remains of the birch, letting it fall onto the ground just within my field of vision. I could see that it had been reduced to but a poor remnant of the thick bundle that had been displayed to my horrified gaze just a bare half hour before, reduced by savage impact with my now reddened and throbbing flesh. I felt Eric's hand on my glowing cheeks and then a soothing coolness as firmly but with great tenderness he applied an antiseptic cream to my bloodied bottom.

'Alice freed my limbs and assisted me to stand while I automatically went through the ritual of thanking my tormentors for inflicting such pain on my poor, tender bottom and acknowledging the good it had, most certainly, done me. When I had finished Alice remarked, "And now I think you would benefit from a little nap, just to restore your energy."

'With that they lead me, still naked, back into the house. Taking every care they tucked me up in their double bed and I soon dozed off in the comforting warmth beneath the thick quilt. I still felt incredibly randy but I was sure that that itch would be scratched soon enough.

'I was not to be disappointed. When I awoke an hour or so later from my healing and refreshing doze, I was still warm and cosy, nestled between the warm and naked flesh of two human beings. I was the meat in a delightful sandwich of sensual humanity.

'Eric's heavy erection burrowed at the cleft between my bum cheeks, the ripe rondure of my buttocks nestling against his groin. One hand was tangled in the luxuriant thatch that sprouted at my Mount, gently kneading my pubis. Alice's left hand rested lightly over my right breast, massaging gently as the pert nipple came awake and ground into the palm of her hand. Her legs twined about mine as we lay together, belly to belly.

'Alice, when she saw that I was awake, released my breast and drew my face towards her own to gently kiss me on the mouth, probing her tongue between my lips where it sucked wetly on my own. I wriggled my bottom against Eric's insistent weapon and felt with satisfaction his semi-hard flesh blossom into full, rock hardness as the plump flesh of my buttocks enfolded him.

'His fingers began to work at my pussy, frigging me to a forgetfulness of my still throbbing nates. Two fingers dipped into my oozing cunt, dabbling in the lake of juices there, then with lazy strokes he spread the musky moisture over my cunt lips and the sensitive clitoral bud. Again and again those magic fingers worked at me - dabble and stroke, dabble and stroke. The electric sensations built in me to an incredible sexual tension. I ground my bum against Eric's belly enthusiastically, the throbbing only serving to heighten my need. Alice bent her head to suckle my breasts, drawing the nipples between sharp, nipping teeth as passion firmed me.

'Over and over Eric's fingers probed my cunt and spread the rich honey spending of my sex to coat my inner thighs, all the while worrying at my clitty until, at last, wave after wave of pure sensation broke over me and I came.

'I was literally sobbing with ecstasy as Eric's firm hands on my shoulders turned me onto my back. I opened my legs and Eric, his full weight bearing on me and crushing me to the mattress, climbed between them and entered me smoothly. I felt his hugeness inside me as he began to fuck me slowly, twisting his weapon with each stroke, our bodies moulding together, my breasts crushed to his powerful chest.

'Still working inside me, he rolled us over so that now I was on top. I sat up astride him as Alice straddled his face and lowered her pussy to his mouth until his tongue entered her and began to slurp at her womanhood. She reached out and grasped my breasts, squeezing and kneading the ripe flesh as I rode up and down on her husband's rock hard maleness.

'Soon we were all coming. Eric, with a grunt of lust, clasped my poor wounded bottom as his manhood throbbed inside me, jetting gouts of his creamy seed into my womb. Alice in her ecstasy rolled from him, dragging me by the bosom down on top of her. And so we lay, a panting, sweating heap of well pleasured humanity.

'We spent the rest of the day in bed, of course. I don't suppose many people can say they had experienced such pleasure (oh, and pain too) as a result of French irregular verbs.'

Wendy closed off in her usual manner, on the one hand, hoping that she had pleased me while on the other, dropping strong hints that she expected to be punished.

Frankly, although her stories were both interesting and stimulating, I was becoming quite frustrated with this experiment in modern communication. Firstly there was lacking for me the tangible and tactile. A punishment is no good unless inflicted in the flesh and on the flesh, in my opinion. Secondly Wendy seemed much too eager to submit to chastisement - without the spice of a little unwillingness, a little distaste on the part of the victim, the sauce of domination tastes very bland. I determined to bring matters to a head and sent this message:

'Wendy, the time has come for you to submit to me in person. You will visit me next weekend and receive whatever punishment I prescribe at my hands and in person. What is it to be? It will be harsh and will tax you to the limit. But you must come here to find out what it is to be.'

I must confess that the reply I received a couple of days later astonished me.

So here I am, sitting at my faithful word-processor, recording the details of my strange correspondence with a young woman called Wendy, to pass the time. Everything is ready, martinet and tawse close to hand, a new school uniform laid out in the bedroom upstairs. If Wendy caught the train we agreed upon that should be her at the door just now ...

## SOMETHING TO CELEBRATE

I was angry. No. I was furious, absolutely livid with rage! Not only had the new computer system been delivered several weeks late, when we did eventually get it the hardware had faults, the programs were full of errors and some of the promised functions didn't work at all. For three weeks my computer department had struggled with these manifold problems and meanwhile the business was being adversely affected, orders were not being shipped, invoices not processed.

The people who supplied the system had worked hard to rectify the problems. We had expected things to go less than smoothly; none of us are exactly innocents and we had made provisions to avert some of the worst effects of the introduction of the new systems. Certainly, a call from me to the supplier's Managing Director had got me all the high-level attention focused on the problems that I could have wished for. What was really annoying me, though, was that during all this time the salesman, or I should say saleswoman, who had sold us the system was noticeable by her absence.

As Chairman and Managing Director of this organisation I, of course, took part in the selection of the new computer system. Quite naturally I let my departmental managers worry about the technical aspects - that is what they are paid for - but the contract and commercial negotiations were up to me. In the course of these protracted discussions I encountered Karen Briggs, our 'account manager'. She is an attractive girl in her mid-twenties, probably with a degree in an obscure subject from an equally obscure university, but overall a typically tenacious sales type on her way to the top. She certainly knew when to treat us all to a flash of her shapely thighs to divert attention when a tricky technical point came up and she was entertaining company over the several lunches and dinners needed to bring negotiations to a head. I must admit that her tenacity in pursuit of the business began to irritate me but in the end her firm won out on technical merit ...

Around here my word is law. When I say 'jump' the only question allowed is, 'How high?' So, getting tired of waiting for Karen to put in an appearance I summoned her to a meeting at my office. She was going to get a piece of my mind and a lecture on my view of professional sales ethics and be made to understand what I expected from an 'account manager' who dealt with my firm. If she was lucky that would be all she would get. But time would tell.

A few minutes later than the appointed time, Penny, my personal assistant, announced my visitor and ushered Ms. Briggs into my office.

"Thank you, Penny." I waved her away. "You can get off home now. But please make sure that everyone knows we are not to be disturbed."

Karen was smartly dressed as ever, in a pale blue business suit with, underneath, a crisp white blouse, primly buttoned to the throat: the uniform of her calling. Complete with Gucci briefcase, she breezed into my office, offering her well-manicured hand in a limp facsimile of the traditional businessman's greeting.

I ushered her to a chair and, from my stronghold behind my polished rosewood desk, I spent the next thirty minutes in lecturing her on my views. Occasionally she tried to break in and offer some remarks which might excuse or explain. I reminded her that she was there to listen and to learn and that, at this point, her opinions were of no value and of less interest. So I carried on, speakinng calmly, not raising my voice, making each point clearly and crisply. I must confess that I was particularly pleased to note that this calm and unemotional approach seemed to be having quite a chilling effect on my victim.

"So," I concluded, "my firm has already lost a large amount of money due to the system you sold to us. You, for your part, seem to have lost interest since we placed the order and that is just not good enough. There will be a claim for damages against your company - a very substantial claim - and your selling methods and personal conduct will be very relevant." Of course, such a claim was highly unlikely to succeed and I had no intention of pursuing one but quite obviously the threat impressed Karen. I licked my lips as I saw her flinch and the colour drain from her checks which had become flushed with embarrassment as I warmed to my lecture. I pressed home my advantage. "Unless," I added, "you care to make some form of personal restitution?"

Her face, framed by her short blonde hair, was now deathly pale. Her tongue played nervously over her dry lips while haunted blue eyes darted from left to right avoiding direct contact with my stern glare.

"What do you mean, res-restitution?" she stammered. Her usual poise had quite deserted her.

In a matter-of-fact voice, as if I were proposing the most obvious and natural solution to a mutual dilemma, I mounted my favourite hobby-horse. "Corporal pun-

47

ishment would probably do you a lot of good. And, my dear, it would also square things quite admirably."

"My God!" she said. "But that's gross - obscene!"

"Not at all," I said. "Only what you deserve. Don't you agree?"

"Well -"

As she hesitated I reached into my desk drawer and tossed my favourite tawse onto the desk in front of Karen's wide-eyed gaze. Her face bore an expression which contained a mixture of apprehension, intrigue and downright disbelief as she eyed the black leather instrument which lay menacingly on the polished desk. Quite obviously she was amazed at the prospect but nevertheless her hand reached out timidly to stroke the strip of leather.

"You - you want to spank me with that?" she finally stammered.

"Yes."

"It's - no! - it's not on. No way!" But she didn't sound very convinced about that.

It was time to drive home my advantage. "So you'd rather lose your job?"

A very curious sort of half smile flitted across her tense face. "Well, if you put it like that ..."

"Oh, I most certainly do put it like that!" I said. "You deserve to be punished and punishment is what you'll get - one way or another."

Cowed, backed into a corner, she tried to hide behind bravado and bluster. "Do your worst then," she spat. "But you really are the worst kind of grubby creep!"

I ignored that. Always concentrate on what matters, and what mattered right then was that I had won. Or nearly won. "Get ready then," I urged.

"I am ready, creep!"

"Oh no. This is a bare bottom affair."

"WHAT!!"

"Yes, Karen, of course. On your bare behind."

She hesitated for a long time. She was on the verge and it could go either way. I imagined the thoughts that must be racing through her mind, balancing a bare assed beating against a bleak future without the job that meant money and status and security. Then her shoulders straightened. "Creep!" she murmured grudgingly through clenched teeth. But from her expression I could tell that I had her beaten.

As if she were in a dream, she got to her feet and reached behind to release her skirt, drawing down the zip, sloughing the garment down her legs and stepping out of it. She had fine legs, very shapely, clad in blue stockings that were held taut by a pastel blue garter belt. My eyes lingered on the scrap of blue nylon lace that concealed, just barely concealed, her pussy.

She hesitated again. "I'll tell you when to stop," I barked at her. "I want you naked!"

She stirred herself again, still in a state of shock, took off her jacket and began to unbutton the blouse. Then the blouse was sliding off her shoulders and down her arms to join the skirt where it lay on the floor. Again she reached behind her to unclip the pastel blue bra that matched her other undergarments. Her firm, ripe breasts tumbled from their captivity; ample gourds of creamy flesh, tipped by rosy nipple buds which bedded in wide aureolae, spilling into view.

She hooked her thumbs into the waistband of her panties and drew them down her legs and over her feet, dropping them to join the heap of her discarded clothing on the floor.

"That will do." I stood back, taking time to run an appreciative eye over her creamy pale body. She crossed futile arms across the swell of her breasts in a vain attempt at modesty but dropped them to her side in obedience to a motion of my hand. I let my gaze dwell on the downy blonde fluff that barely covered her pubis before lifting my eyes to candidly admire her breasts yet again.

I was pleased to note that the colour had really mounted to her cheeks. She was blushing a deep, deep red of embarrassment and humiliation.

I came out from behind my desk and picked up the tawse, flexing the supple leather beneath her astounded gaze. Clearly she could not yet quite believe that this was happening to her, did not know whether to run or stay, still did not quite know whether she would allow this to happen to her.

I did not give her time for further inner debate but got down to work! I made her bend over the edge of the desk with her head cradled in the crook of her folded arms. Her bare and delectably rounded buttocks were thus presented for punishment, thrust pertly in the air to receive a proper, old-fashioned pasting. Her breasts dangled heavily beneath her and swayed gently from side to side with her breathing.

I stood behind my recumbent victim and let my hand run luxuriously over the silk smooth skin of her firm posteriors as I made minor adjustments to her positioning. Then 'thwaaak!' I unleashed the tawse, smacking the leather squarely across the plumpest portion of her bum.

She almost jumped upright with the shock. A gasp of pain escaped her lips and a grimace of pain contorted her charming features. A distinct red area formed on the white, almost translucent, buttock flesh.

I drew back and 'whaaak!', again the supple leather connected with Karen's taut bottom. She shuddered, which made her dangling titties dance delightfully. I laid on harder and really punished her as her quivering bum flesh took on a deep red hue. Soon her entire rear end was glowing hotly red while her whole being became centred on the pain in her bum. At first she suffered silently but as the strokes loaded pain on pain she began to groan and whimper.

Suddenly, just as I was getting into my stride, there came a sharp knock at the door. I put up the tawse but motioned to Karen that she was to stay where she was, bent over the desk with her throbbing arse in the air. I slipped out of the office, pulling the door to behind me.

It was Tom, the manager of the computer department. We exchanged a few words and he gave me a quick briefing on the current situation.

A few moments later, having fixed a grim look on my face, I entered my office again. Karen was still bent over the desk, her fiery bumcheeks aglow and did I detect the telltale shine of the track of a single tear on her left cheek?

"More grief with the damn computer!" I remarked sorrowfully. "You really are in for it now!"

I took up the tawse once more and really began to leather poor Karen's defenceless arse, slapping the leather hard against her bumcheeks, relieving my frustrations on them. Karen jigged from one leg to the other, whimpering and groaning while her pretty face contorted with pain.

Finally I grew tired of this exercise and tossed the well used tawse onto the desk in front of the poor tortured girl. Again I told her not to stir and moved into her line of sight so that she could see just what was going on. I locked the office door, making quite a production of the elaborate use of the key and sliding home the bolts top and bottom - I didn't want any more interruptions. Then, very deliberately and without any undue haste, I began to remove my own clothes. Soon I was naked with my male member standing heavily erect and jutting fiercely out from below my belly.

"What is it now?" Karen asked nervously as, head still cradled on her arms, she watched me strip for action.

"No questions. Your place is to obey and not to ask foolish questions."

Once more I stood behind her and made her part her thighs so that the entrance to her cunt was revealed in all its pinkly moist glory. I ran my hands over the hotly glowing globes of her posteriors kneading the flesh until she yelped. Then, placing the head of my engorged manhood between her pussy lips I thrust home to embed myself deeply in her cunt which, not greatly to my surprise was sopping wet and ready to receive me. She half twisted herself round to face me, a look of disbelief on her face. The words of a half-hearted protest died on her lips as my belly slapped against her bum cheeks and Karen let out a low moan which could have been a groan of pain but was more likely a gasp of pleasure.

I remained quite still with my prick clasped in Karen's sex. I reached around her to seize a dangling breast in each hand and roughly kneaded the yielding silky sacs. I squeezed hard on the ripe flesh, mashing her tits against her rib cage, then, moulding the plastic flesh I drew my grasp down until I held her by the nipple buds between thumb and forefinger. Despite herself Karen was becoming increasingly excited by this treatment, her nipples were lust engorged berries in my grasp, her pussy flooded with her juices which welled around the throbbing root of my penis as she wriggled her silk smooth nates against me and purred lustfully.

Still motionless and fixed in her up to the root, I pinched both nipples as hard as I could, increasing the pressure, harder and harder. Deep in her throat Karen moaned at the pain I was making in her abused titflesh, but the muscles of her cunt clasping on my prick and the squirming of her bum against my belly told me that she did not want me to stop.

With a parting squeeze, I let go of her bosom and instead grasped her hips firmly. I began to fuck in and out of her sex. Slowly I withdrew along the length of her sopping wet tunnel feeling her cunt walls lovingly clasping my erect length until just the tip penetrated her pussy. Then, equally slowly, I pushed back in, reaming her sex to probe her cunt womb deep. In and out of her sex I fucked while my hands dug roughly into Karen's fair skinned flesh.

It was quite obvious by her reaction that my victim was beginning to thrive under this treatment. Each inward thrust brought a yelp of pleasure as her bum thrust back at me to aid and deepen my penetration. Her eyes were tight shut and her tongue played moistly over her lips. Now her moans were quite clearly moans of pleasure as my male hardness filled her up. She was on the brink of a glorious, shuddering orgasm, within a few strokes of the abyss.

Suddenly I left off fucking, allowing my tool to slip from her oozing hole with a slight 'plop'. It hung at my groin, shining with a liberal coating of Karen's love juices as Karen gasped and a sigh of quite obvious disappointment escaped her lips.

"On your knees." I ordered. Obediently she raised herself from the desk and knelt before me. I presented my still unsatisfied erection to her lips and ordered her to lick it clean.

Eagerly, her eyes still glazed with lust, she reached up to cradle my scrotum on one hand, feeling the generous weight of my seed purse. With her other hand she delicately steadied the shaft, putting out her pink tongue to lick the crown with relish, laving it with her spittle before running her tongue over the ridge of the glans and thence down the entire length to bury her nose in my pubic beard. Then she was licking the heavily erect shaft as if it were a giant lollipop, adding her saliva to the musky coating left by her own sex cavern.

I let her carry on for a while, enjoying the sensations her tongue produced in my manhood, watching her blonde head bobbing about. Then I stopped her and grasping the sides of her head, thrust my entire length into her mouth until the crown hit the back of her throat. She gagged, then opened her throat and with bulging cheeks accommodated herself to receive me.

"Suck me!" I began to fuck in and out of her mouth just as I had used her cunt, while her carmined lips sucked wetly at my shaft. The girl sucked bravely as I violated her mouth, forcing her jaws open with my prick, ramming my meat into her throat.

When my seed boiled in my balls I did not think of holding back but with a grunt of animal lust let it rush along my excited length to erupt into Karen's mouth. A copious jet of hot cream boiled out of my pulsing weapon to hit the back of her throat and fill her mouth to over-flowing. I pulled my prick from her flooded mouth as she fought to swallow down my spending, flecks of come trickling at the corner of her mouth and down her chin.

I directed my member as a second and a third jet of creamy jism spurted from me to splash squarely in Karen's face and over her heaving tits. Her tongue lapped around her lips as the thick cream slithered down her face to pool at her collar bone. Absently, her hand spread the semen over her body and massaged it into the flesh of her bosom.

She had understood by now that she must not move until she was told. She just knelt there with my seed drying on her face and chest while I got dressed again.

"Now Karen, I think it would help customer relations if we met more regularly. You will have lunch with me here every Wednesday - plan to spend at least two hours. Now get your clothes and get out."

Her response, although unexpected and surprising from one whom I had counted inexperienced in such matters as we had just then explored, was nonetheless highly gratifying. Still kneeling, a slight smile playing about those enticing, lips she quietly replied:

"Thank you, er, Sir, for showing me my errors. I shall look forward to our meetings in the future."

And the girl actually meant it! She even managed a cheeky wink as she got to her feet and used my private bathroom to clean herself up.

When she had gone I picked up the phone.

"Tom, thanks for letting me know that everything is up and working. It's great news. What say you and your team meet me for drinks in Rubens Bar in fifteen minutes. I was a little busy when you came up but now I think we've all got something to celebrate!"

## THE GAME

Friday evening! Ever since George had announced over dinner on Monday that Friday was to be a 'Games Night' the coming of the weekend had loomed before Jenny, threatening but also perversely exciting. She had known better than to ask what game George had in mind. She knew that she had been especially naughty this time. That dress had been very extravagant and then she had arrived home late from her shopping trip and the meal hadn't been ready when George came home. Whatever her husband had in mind it was bound to be something unpleasant. But Jenny knew she would have to suffer whatever indignity he had planned for her without demur.

When George arrived home from the office he was wearing a quiet smile of anticipation. He always enjoyed these little games. He must have been looking forward to this evening's sport with particular relish.

Jenny stood before him, her head bowed and her hands clasped behind her back, as he lounged in the armchair and reminded her of her misdemeanours and told her exactly what was in store for her as a consequence. As he spoke Jenny's legs turned to water and her stomach churned as if a thousand butterflies had suddenly taken off in there.

It seemed that George planned to take her to a certain public house a couple of miles away. They wouldn't exactly be going together. Jenny was to enter first, George would follow a little later and watch the fun unfold from some vantage point. Inside, Jenny was to seek out any man who might be on his own and, to be blunt, pick him up. Later she would persuade him to come back to the house with her. George didn't need to go into further detail, Jenny knew well enough what was to happen after that.

As she listened, the first shocked reaction began to wear off and Jenny began to reflect on the intriguing possibilities that the little escapade contained. She found herself becoming quite excited. She just knew she was becoming moist between her thighs in anticipation, could almost feel the telltale dampness spreading to her panties.

Of course, she told herself, George would have hand picked the man she was to meet. The stranger would be no stranger at all but one of George's cronies. The experience would be humiliating enough. George would have seen to that. If nothing else there would be the embarrassment of making the first approach, the possibility of getting the wrong man.

"Time to go and make yourself beautiful," George concluded. "And don't forget, you must be especially nice to him. Make him want to come back with you."

Upstairs George went straight into the bedroom, leaving Jenny to take her shower in the bathroom.

She ran the water to heat up while she stripped off her daytime clothes and placed them in the wash basket. The water was just right when she stepped under the spray. She let the hot jets of water play invigoratingly over her skin for a while then soaped herself carefully. She let the shower play over her body for a little longer, rinsing herself off, before stepping out and towelling herself dry.

Naked, she padded across the landing and entered the bedroom.

George had already picked out what she was to wear and had laid it out on the bed. No underwear, Jenny noted without surprise, no bra, no panties.

George was sitting on the bed with his back propped against the headboard ready to supervise Jenny's preparations.

"Wear some of that perfume," he said, pointing to a small bottle, half filled with an amber liquid, that stood on the dressing table.

Jenny picked up the bottle and used the cut glass stopper to dab a little of the sweet smelling contents between her full breasts. She drew the stopper down her body to her navel, trailing a damp line of perfume over her skin. She drew more from the bottle, smearing it over her abdomen just above the rich tuft of curls that adorned her pubis. The citron odour of bergamot hung in the air.

"Good. Now your makeup. Nice rich red lips. Blusher for your cheeks and just a hint of eye-shadow to bring out the hazel in your eyes."

Jenny sat at the dressing table, pausing to inspect her full, rounded breasts, before applying the makeup exactly as her husband had instructed. She ran a brush through her straight, auburn hair, flicking the ends pertly upwards just below her jaw line. Finished, she turned towards George, seeking his approval.

"That's fine. Now get dressed. The stockings first."

Jenny drew the sheer black stockings over her legs, fixing them in place with the plain elastic garters she had found beside them. She put on the cream silk blouse that, when buttoned, fitted snugly over her firm bosom. The open neck plunged deeply to reveal a goodly expanse of ivory white throat and the cleft between the plumpness of her breasts which were held bunched together by the tight material.

It was a button-through skirt. When Jenny put it on it swirled full and loose just below her knees but by leaving two or three buttons unfastened there would be opportunity to show off her attractive legs when she sat. George had no need to point this out.

It only remained for her to put on the shiny patent leather, high heeled shoes that George had selected and the game could begin in earnest.

Outside the pub Jenny paced up and down trying to get her quaking nerves under control. She took a deep breath, pushed open the door and stepped inside. Her pulse was racing and her breath was coming in quick, shallow draughts as she walked across to the bar with her gaze fixed straight ahead.

The place wasn't very busy and the barman served her straightaway. Jenny took her glass and retreated to a table in a dimly lit corner to recruit her wits and look around the bar room.

She unbuttoned her overcoat and slipped it from her shoulders. She noted with relief that the chill night air had had no apparent effect on her nipples. To have to sit there, on display, with such an obvious indication that beneath the tight fabric of her blouse her breasts were bare would have been too embarrassing. But to have sat there wrapped in her coat would not have been acceptable to George.

She was meant to be on display.

Sipping her drink and looking about her, she found to her annoyance that her hastily chosen vantage point only allowed her to see about one half of the room. A wooden partition and a coat rack obscured the rest of the bar from her view. In the area she could see, no obvious candidate for her attentions presented himself. There were a pair of young girls, probably secretaries from one of the nearby offices, having a drink at the bar with their equally youthful boyfriends. Another man and a woman sat at a table close by. A couple of older men, in animated conversation, lounged in the corner of the bar. No single man though.

George came in and walked across to the bar with barely a glance in Jenny's direction. Although she had never been to this pub before it was quite obvious that George was a regular. The barman came straight over to him with a welcoming word. He even seemed to know what George wanted to drink without prompting. George climbed on to a high stool at the corner of the bar from where he could command a view of the whole room, including Jenny tucked away in her shadowy nook. The two bar side loungers joined him and embraced him in their conversation.

Jenny sipped her drink. Minutes passed as she scanned the thinly populated room. Still no lone male came into view. Suddenly she became aware of George making subtle gestures with his head in her direction. They seemed to be becoming more urgent as she seemingly failed to catch on to what he was trying to signal. She followed the direction of his glance and understood. She smiled an acknowledgement. Of course, the target George had set up for the game must have been sitting out of her view, beyond the wooden partition. But George had spotted him.

Jenny drained her glass and walked over to the bar to buy a refill. Now that George was here and she was about to see her companion for the evening she felt calmer. While the barman mixed her drink she glanced about her, trying to locate her intended partner.

When she saw him her sigh of relief was almost audible. George hadn't let her down. The man, sitting alone at a table at the back of the room, was quite presentable really. His hair, brownish and receding a little, was swept back across his head. His nose was a little too big and his lips a little too full for Jenny's taste, but on the whole not bad looking in a mid-forties, lived in sort of way. Well dressed too, in a dark pin-striped suit as if he had just come from the office.

"Do you mind if I sit here?"

The man looked up from his newspaper. He'd been tackling that day's crossword while he waited. He returned Jenny's smile, murmured, "No, no. Not at all," and went back to his paper.

Jenny sat down in the vacant seat across the table from the man. She sipped her drink and he seemed to ignore her, still gripped by his crossword. Jenny felt George's eyes on her, urging her to get on with it. She glanced in his direction. His look was eloquent. This wasn't being made any easier for her.

"Have you come straight from the office?" she found herself saying in the absence of a better inspiration.

The man looked up. "Mm, yes. Just dropped in on my way home."

Jenny noticed the tang of the cologne he was wearing. One of her favourites; George sometimes used it. Now that she had his attention she knew she must use the opportunity.

"I like a drink to unwind at the end of the day too."

The man nodded and returned some inconsequential remark.

"Crosswords are quite relaxing," Jenny pursued. "I used to be quite good at them. Do you mind if I help?"

It got easier after that. From discussing the clues which he read out to her, their conversation developed, ranging over several social topics. Casually Jenny leaned back in her seat, crossing her legs, letting her skirt slip open to show off her plump knees and three or four inches of tempting thigh. The man began to really pay attention to her now. Jenny saw him look appreciatively at her shapely calf, caressed by the clinging web of transparent black nylon. She experienced a tiny frisson of pleasure as his gaze wandered higher to settle longingly on her black clad thigh.

The man drained his glass and asked, "Can I get you another?"

Jenny smiled acceptance. "Yes. Thank you. A white wine spritzer, please," and she held out her empty glass.

"By the way, I'm Tom," he said as he took it from her.

"Hello Tom, I'm Jenny," and she held out her hand for him to clasp briefly.

While he was at the bar Jenny loosened another of the buttons, carefully arranging the skirt to reveal the whole expanse of her stockinged thigh and just a hint, the tiniest hint, of the soft, white flesh above. She glanced in George's direction and saw his slight nod of approval.

When Tom got back it was clear that Jenny's rearrangement of her clothing had had the desired effect. He stooped over her just a little longer than was absolutely necessary as he set down her glass, taking in the creamy smooth expanse of her cleavage. As they drank and chatted his gaze kept returning to her legs.

After a while Jenny became aware that George had left. It was time to be going. She drained her glass and, as casually as she could, said:

"I think I've had all the white wine and soda water I need for one night. If you could offer a lady a lift home I'd be glad to provide coffee, or something better, when we got there. You have a car?"

Tom seemed to be playing his part to the hilt. The look on his face showed that he could hardly believe his luck. He stammered as he agreed that, yes, he had a car and would be delighted to provide a lift. It even seemed to Jenny that his hands were trembling as he helped her on with her coat.

Tom's car was parked in the furthest, darkest corner of the pub's car park. In the front seat Jenny slipped her coat from her shoulders. She was pleased now to see that her nipples were clearly visible, pushing like hard buds against the thin silk of her blouse, stiffened by the cold and by her own growing arousal. That should be a clear sign to her new found friend, if he should need one.

"Be nice to him," George had said. Jenny stretched out her hand, placing it in Tom's lap, feeling the outline of his resting penis beneath her palm. She tilted her head up to him, offering her mouth. He bent, kissing her lips. Her mouth worked on him and Jenny was soon welcoming the intrusion of his exploring tongue. She took his hand and placed it on her thigh above the line of her stocking.

It was a nice kiss. Jenny was enjoying the feel of his hand as it caressed the plump moistness of her inner thighs. She would gladly have climbed into the back seat and let him take her there and then but she knew George would want to see everything. Squeezing Tom's hand between her thighs she whispered in his ear,

"Mmm, that's nice. But we'll be much more comfortable at my house."

With Jenny directing they were soon there. The lights burning behind the front room curtains told her that George was already inside, ready and waiting.

She ushered Tom through the hall and into the lounge. She was most impressed by his acting skills when he came face to face with George who was sprawled in his favourite armchair. From the look of confusion on Tom's face, reminding her of a frightened rabbit caught in the lights of an oncoming car, she could almost let herself believe that he had not been expecting to find her husband there. George took charge straightaway.

"Come in old chap. Make yourself at home," gesturing to another armchair which was drawn up beside his own. "Jenny, get our friend a drink. Would Scotch be alright?"

Jenny fetched them both a tumbler of whiskey and stood back waiting instructions. George sipped his drink and spoke again.

"Come along then Jenny, take off your clothes and show our friend what a charming body you have for him."

Tom's eyes goggled as Jenny's fingers worked at the buttons of her blouse which she stripped off to give him his first glimpse of her splendidly firm young bosom. She loosed the waistband of her skirt and let it fall about her feet. She hesitated, looking enquiringly at George who nodded imperceptibly, then bent to roll down and remove her stockings before standing, stark naked, her hands at her side so that Tom could get a good look at her.

"She's got a delightful figure, don't you think?" George drawled. "Her breasts are especially fine - perfect tear-drops, and so ripely elastic. Her belly too. Flat with just a hint of swell below the navel."

Jenny felt herself colouring up. She would never get used to George discussing her body so intimately with strangers. George was still talking while Tom seemed mesmerised by the sight of Jenny's creamy smooth flesh.

"You know, Jenny has been rather naughty recently. I've been meaning to punish her myself. Perhaps you'd care to do the honours? Jenny, run along and fetch the cane."

Jenny didn't need to go far. Just to the corner of the lounge where an umbrella stand held a selection of such instruments. She selected an especially whippy rattan and was back, standing in her place, holding it loosely in her hand, in a second or two. Tom seemed to find his voice.

"Er, er, no. No thank you. If you don't mind. I don't think so."

Jenny, despite the trepidation she usually felt in the face of a caning, experienced a twinge of disappointment. George seemed not to have chosen very wisely this time. Although she couldn't say she actually enjoyed being caned she had to admit that the effect afterwards was worth a sore bottom. The effect on George too made it worthwhile. Apparently, though, they were both to be disappointed tonight. George, however, did not seem to put out as he continued breezily,

"Whatever you wish. We'll just keep this handy in case you change your mind." He relieved Jenny of the cane. "Now this lovely girl is at your complete disposal. Do whatever you like to her. See! Here are a pair of delicious breasts just crying out to be squeezed, nipples aching to be tweaked and nibbled."

At last Tom seemed to be entering into the spirit of things. Laying his glass aside he got to his feet and, with his gaze still fixed on her invitingly nude body, crossed the few feet of carpet to where Jenny stood. Once more she tilted her head, offering her mouth to him. As his tongue slipped between her parted lips his hand went to her breast, moulding the resilient flesh. He squeezed gently, feeling the warm plumpness ooze between his fingers. He lowered his mouth, suckling on the nipples that had magically hardened into fat, round acorns. His tongue rasped over white flesh, coating Jenny's skin with a shiny trail of saliva as the first twinges of arousal flowed through her.

His hand slipped down her spine and over the rondure of her buttocks. He stroked, caressed, probing fingers tentatively exploring the furrow between bum cheeks. He lifted his head to look Jenny in the face.

"You know, I think I'll change my mind. Where's that cane?"

"Bravo," boomed George. "I knew you wouldn't be able to resist her plump little arse. I usually give her twelve. That's usually sufficient. Jenny, you know what you have to do. Get yourself ready."

Jenny moved eagerly to place a couple of cushions and then lay herself over the padded arm of the sofa so that her well fleshed rump was positioned to receive the stinging strokes of the cane. It seemed that Tom's initial reluctance had just been another ploy to tease her. Another subtle tug at the strings of her emotions. Now she was to get the full treatment she so urgently craved. Her blood pounded as the sexual tension built satisfyingly within her.

Tom fumbled the first couple of strokes. They landed imprecisely, stinging but without making the deep and lasting impression that was desired. Jenny heard a muffled conversation take place behind her; George giving Tom the benefit of his considerable experience.

After that things got along much better. The next stroke cracked crisply athwart the very apex of Jenny's smooth, ivory posteriors. The pain was intense, jerking Jenny's head back with the shock and making her howl out loud. But after the pain she felt the heat, the sexual warmth flowing from the point of impact to her sex.

Tom plied the rod steadily, leaving plenty of time between each stroke for both victim and her tormentors to savour the effects. Jenny's plump bum flesh quivered under each new assault and she yelled lustily but all the while the deep warmth was spreading within her. When Tom applied the final stroke, a cut across the juicy tops of her thighs which would remind her of the evening for the rest of the week, Jenny was thoroughly aroused.

Glancing back over her shoulder through the salty tears that had started spontaneously in her eyes, she glimpsed her bottom glowing a fiery, satisfying crimson. Her sex, she knew, was liquid desire, the honey thick juice seeping between the lips of her pussy.

Over her shoulder she also saw Tom approaching. He was naked now. His body, hairless but for a sparse mat of grizzled hair over the chest, was quite attractive, taut apart from a slight paunch. His penis, though, was very interesting; not especially long, but thick as a woman's wrist and jutting stiff and proud beneath his belly, erupting from a mane of pubic hair.

Jenny turned away as his hands cupped her buttocks, making them sting anew. She felt the tip of his erection being rubbed over her smooth bum cheeks to smear a trail of the oily seminal fluid that oozed from the eyelet. Then his fingers were inside her cunt, paddling freely in the liberally flowing juices, spreading her musky fragrant love liquor up over her perineum, over her fesses, even dampening the furrow between her bum cheeks.

A thick forefinger probed at the tightly muscled ring of her anus, stretching her, lubricating her. She shuddered pleasurably. He was going to bugger her. Jenny loved being taken in the arse, but right now she had a more urgent need. She had a hungry pussy that needed feeding. She wanted his thick, hard meat rammed in her quim, wanted to feel his flesh forcing the walls of her vagina apart.

Her relief was almost palpable when she felt his fingers part her pussy lips, felt him lodge the head of his penis between them. Slowly he fed himself into her letting her feel every inch slither inside her until she felt his belly slap against her bum.

He began to work in her, building the pace until he was rogering her madly. His hands roved over her body, finding her breasts, squeezing the flesh, rolling the rock hard nipples between thumb and forefinger. She sighed happily as he slipped a hand down between the cushions and her groin to find and manipulate her clitoris which seemed to swell under his touch.

Jenny was groaning and sighing in abandon, bucking her body to meet Tom's thrusts. The flood of bliss surged inside her like an ocean roller, gathering momentum until she came in a long drawn out, howling, squealing climax. So intense was her orgasm that she barely noticed Tom's body stiffen as he poured a long stream of semen into her womb.

Jenny was sitting up in bed, propped against the pillows, drowsing and letting her mind wander in free-flow over the events of the evening. Her bottom still tingled from the punishment she had received. Her nipples ached where eager fingers had tweaked and mouths sucked. Her well used sex was sore. But she was cocooned in a warm blanket of sexual contentment. She was blissfully happy.

After that first frenzied coupling Tom had seemed to lose all his inhibitions and really entered into the spirit of things. He was soon erect again and having lavished attention on her breasts and quim with his mouth he had taken Jenny in the arse, buggering her vigorously. Then George had deigned to join them.

The two men used Jenny between them, driving her to the very edge of bliss then holding back while they treated the jiggling cheeks of her bottom to a crisp spanking. This process was repeated again and again until none of them could hold back longer and all three plunged into the orgasmic maelstrom

Tom had finally left about two in the morning and George had brought Jenny upstairs for a final romp on the bed before settling down for sleep.

George stirred beside her, making himself comfortable. At least, Jenny thought, tomorrow they could sleep until noon. Then George would probably bring breakfast in bed to be followed by an afternoon of gentle, sensual love making. George was always especially solicitous after a game when Jenny had pleased him particularly.

Dreamily Jenny murmured,

"So where do you know Tom from? The office?"

George rolled towards her, his face suddenly lit up by a broad grin of amusement.

"Tom? I don't know him from Adam," he chuckled. "But in all the excitement I quite forgot about poor old Charlie Barnes. He must have gone to the wrong pub - probably still sitting there. Or got cold feet and didn't show up."

Jenny felt the hot flush of embarrassment rise up again, her cheeks glowing as George dissolved into ribald laughter.

# INTO THE FIRE

The chill evening air raised goose bumps on Jayne's skin as she climbed out of the taxi. She paid the driver and watched as the black, boxy London cab drew away from the kerb and drove off, leaving her alone. The late evening streets were empty now, the shops and offices closed and deserted. A gust of wind blew a sheet of discarded newspaper against the doorway of a shop which was displaying a prominent 'To Let' sign. Evening was drawing on into night and soon the blue twilight gloom would turn to inky black darkness.

High heels clicking on the pavement, teetering slightly on the five inch stilettoes, she made her way towards the entrance to the shopping mall.

'How odd I must look,' she thought, 'carrying my coat over my arm in this evening chill. And dressed like this too.' But there was no one else about to see her. The strangeness was only apparent to herself.

Inside, the shopping mall was empty of life just like the street outside. Jayne's footsteps echoed as if in the great, empty, vaulted space of some cathedral. She strode on, becoming used to the high heels, on past the still lighted windows of a chain store, past the bowl of a fountain, now waterless and inactive, and on past the brutal modernist bronze sculpture that stood at the heart of the precinct.

She caught a glimpse of herself in the plain mirrored glass decorating a shop front. 'Nice legs,' she thought absently. Yes, her legs had always been one of her best features. Long and shapely. Clad in the black stockings, black nylon moulding calves and firmly contoured thighs, they were at their best. The short skirt showed off an inviting portion of those thighs; not enough to be blatant but sufficient to hold out a wealth of sexy promise. The extraordinarily high heels played their part too, turning ankle and calf and making those legs seem even longer.

Her attention caught by her own reflection, she gazed at herself mirrored in the shop doorway. She looked her fill at those fine legs. Then her gaze travelled upwards, past the short skirt, past her nipped in waist, over the shot-silk blouse, open at the neck, and past the understated rope of pearls that twined at her throat. Her breasts too were another pleasing feature, full and ripe. She could just discern a hint of cleavage where the half cups of her bra held them high to thrust pertly against the silk.

Her lingering gaze had travelled upwards. She was not sure about her makeup. Not quite her usual low-key look. Sexy. It was definitely sexy but certainly not tarty. Her wide, full lipped mouth was well rouged, the crimson lipstick making her lips seem more than usually luscious. Her eyes were widened, emphasised by highlights and subtle use of eye-shadow. Her cheek bones were brought to prominence by use of blusher. Did she like her hair like that? Swept back from her face and held in a pony tail with a bow atop her head?

Time was getting on now and she was expected. She tore herself away from the narcissistic contemplation of her own image and started off again towards the car park.

She soon reached the short, dark tunnel that led there. Suddenly she was overcome by doubt. She shivered involuntarily and not from the cold. Should she keep her appointment? Was it wise? Was it safe?

If it hadn't been for George - dear, kind, polite, gentle, boring George - she would never have looked at those magazines. Never looked in search of excitement, in search of a lover who could thrill her like her poor, dull, gentle husband never could.

Probably she had found sex with George exciting once but she couldn't quite remember such a time. She loved him, of course, and she had married him. Certainly she had found his old-fashioned consideration for her needs refreshing after some of the more selfish and inept men she had known. But now that same consideration had become mechanical and lack-lustre. Every time, George worked diligently at her, using lips and tongue and fingers to bring her to a climax. He held himself back until she was satisfied before climbing between her legs to relieve himself within her. But she was not satisfied! She craved excitement, craved an abandon that would take both her and her partner crashing into the abyss. She wanted to be used ...

As soon as she had seen the advert - a few short lines, crisp and to the point, the extraordinary hidden among the mundane calls for 'sexy woman to make threesome,' and 'toy-boy for daytime fun' - she had known it was speaking to her.

'Step into the flames,' it had urged, 'find the excitement you crave. Your deepest fantasy made real. Place yourself in my hands.'

No, she did not want to be wise or to be safe. She wanted to be taken, to be used, to submit. She strode into the dark tunnel and on into the now empty car park. Her shoes scraped on the rough concrete as she emerged from the clinging darkness.

The car stood exactly where it was supposed to be, right in the middle of the gloomy car park. It was the only vehicle there. It was long and low, a classic phallic symbol crafted in steel and rubber and plastic. An icon of male sexuality painted flame red. The windows were black, opaque. Was there someone inside, waiting for her, watching her approach?

Jayne had dashed off a reply to the box number quoted without pause for thought, pouring intimate details of her frustrations and desires onto paper for nameless strangers to read. In return she had received detailed and explicit instructions - where to come, how to dress.

Finding most of her outfit had been easy. She had had to search a little to find a black half-cup bra that fastened at the front but even this came to hand in a little lingerie boutique that she sometimes used. But those blasted shoes. Black patent with stiletto heels, at least five inches. Then she had recalled another advert in the magazines and so another problem was solved.

Her makeup and even her perfume were all specified in the letter. The time and date too were set down for her. No hint that the appointment might be negotiable - rather a command. There was also a car key; for this car she now stood beside. 'Open the door, climb in and wait,' she had been commanded.

She had had her first crisis of confidence then. How could she contrive to get out for the evening? What excuse could she give to George that would let her stay out half the night, dressed so provocatively? George relieved her of the burden and unwittingly stiffened her resolve when he announced, that same evening, that he would be away on business for the whole of the week in the middle of which her appointment was fixed.

She inserted the key in the lock and had to jump back as the gull-wing door flipped open. The passenger compartment was empty. Jayne stowed her folded coat behind the seat and climbed in, reaching up to pull down and close the door.

The seat was low and moulded about her body, holding her rigid, half reclining, half sitting. She felt her breathing quicken, could hear her heartbeat in the silence. She closed her eyes, just for a second, to calm herself. When she opened them again he was there, standing in front of the sloping bonnet, seeming to look directly at her. He was tall, slim, almost gaunt, dressed in a sort of leather overall or jump suit that clung to his spare frame.

He came around to the side, opened the driver's door and climbed in, pulling it shut behind him in a single, sinuous motion. His hair was close cropped and seemed to be made of the same leather that encased his body, black with a dull sheen. He looked at Jayne with piercing, expressionless, blue eyes - dead and ice cold - mimicking the appraisal she had made of herself just a few minutes before.

Without a word he placed a hand on one rounded knee, stroking the black, taut stretched nylon, moulding her dimpled kneecap in his palm. Lightly his fingers played over her lower thigh, ranging between her knee and the hem of her skirt, seeming to enjoy the texture of the stockings. Gradually his hand worked higher, his eyes still fixing hers, until he encountered bare, smooth flesh above the stocking tops. His open palm caressed silken skin, gently parting her legs to feel the moist plumpness of her inner thigh before worming beneath the taut elastic of suspenders, probing under the nylon sheath.

Already Jayne was feeling quite heated and she began to wriggle under the insistent stroking. She started to whimper pleasurably. Firmly he pinched the flesh of her inner thigh, stilling her instantly.

His hand worked even higher to encounter the lace frilled edging of her black silk french knickers. Still enjoying her rich smoothness, his hand delved into one wide knicker leg, working inwards, finding the mat of her pubic bush.

The skirt was rucked up around her waist to fully expose her lower limbs to his unemotional gaze. Fingers hooked in the waistband of the knickers. Jayne lifted herself and with a single sweeping motion he drew the batiste garment down over her legs and off, to be discarded. His fingers again went to her sex, opening her, probing inside her already liquid cunt. Soon his whole hand was working in her, spreading her juices over her nether lips and inner thigh - finding and working the sensitive nub of her clitoris.

Thrilling to the bizarre situation Jayne rode on wave after wave of sensation that rose from her pussy and broke over her. She couldn't keep still and silent now, had to writhe against the lovely digits that pleasured her so completely. And thus she was lifted to a thundering climax, drumming her heels on the floor of the car as she squeezed the stranger's hand between her thighs.

Her head cleared to find his fingers, smeared with her sweet sour juices, busy at the buttons of her blouse. He pushed it open to reveal the firm flesh of her breasts overflowing the delicate half-cup bra. He bent his head and with lizard tongue licked along her cleavage, dampening the smooth, milky mound with a trail of saliva. With one hand he released the clasp and peeled the cups away from the ripe fruit, baring her to him.

He cupped one breast in his palm, grinding the nipple, pushing it back into the doughy mound. His hand kneaded the tit, squeezing and drawing the flesh into a tautly perfect cone only to release it while he attended to its twin. With hand and mouth, lips and teeth he enjoyed her succulent fleshy orbs, working her again to a fever pitch of excitement.

With a smooth and rapid movement he swung his body over the low control console which separated the seats to kneel between her still parted thighs. With deft movements he opened a panel in his leather suit, releasing his erect member which tumbled out of its confinement, glaring crimson and angry at Jayne's sex with its one eye.

Strong fingers opened her and with a single, smooth movement he was fixed in her, lunging into her liquid sex. He grasped her buttocks, pulling her onto him as his hugeness threatened to split her. Leather ground against soft yielding flesh. His weapon reamed her sodden sex channel as Jayne held herself motionless, being used like a semi-naked, life-sized doll.

Releasing her buttocks he continued to slam in and out of her clinging sex. Placing his hands on her shoulders he forced her down into her seat. He thrust home and Jayne's glutinous sex clasped him as the ripples of release spread through her. His throbbing penis exploded, spewing hot liquid deep inside her. He leaned back, still in her, still spending and slapped her full in the face. The stinging blow merely served to heighten her release and was hardly felt as she squealed from the bottom of her lungs.

Without ceremony or soft words he slipped from her, smearing her pubis and thighs with a residue of his cream and secured his tool, still semi hard, within his leather carapace.

"Cover yourself," came the harsh, gravelled whisper, and Jayne, hands trembling in the aftershock of violent passion, hurried to obey. She fished under the seat for her discarded panties and drew them over her bottom feeling them become damp and clinging from the moisture that oozed from her sex. Quickly she replaced the bra and buttoned her blouse.

The man leaned over and placed a blindfold over her eyes, fastening the velcro straps beneath her ponytail. It was very efficient, shutting out the light completely and plunging her into darkness.

The powerful engine came to life with a throaty growl which settled down to a dull, pulsing throb. Jayne lurched forward as her companion let in the clutch and was jerked back in her seat as the car surged forward. She felt the bump as they bounced over the lip of the ramp leading down to the street. Then all was smoothness and they drove with no sensation of motion except occasionally when in turning a tight corner Jayne was pressed to one side or the other of the constricting seat.

Deprived of vision and of all other sensations of the world outside Jayne withdrew into herself. They could have travelled for hours or for minutes. It did not matter. She had already entered the fantasy world where time and place were of no consequence, where all that mattered was what was done to her body and the sensations that that produced.

Her conscious being was already a delicious, intoxicated turmoil of feeling and emotions. At her core was the warm afterglow that had followed on from sexual release. At the edges of consciousness though there was apprehension, even adrenaline pumping fear. Just how far would they go? What was going to happen to her now? But overarching all, there was the stupendous feeling of being utterly powerless, of being used and controlled that she knew now she had craved for so long.

The car stopped abruptly and she was shaken from her day-dream state. She felt cold air as the car door opened. A hand took her by the upper arm - a tight grip, fingers digging into muscle and flesh - and led her from the car, along a path, through doors, along corridors. She crossed a floor that seemed strangely padded, which did not scrape or echo to her footfall and was brought to a stand, still on the cushioned surface.

"Let's see her then." The voice, distant and muffled but not the leather man's whispered rasp.

Ungentle hands opened the blouse, tearing it, ripping at the buttons. It was pushed over her shoulders and off. The bra was unclasped and peeled off, leaving her breasts to swing free, full and round. The skirt followed. She stepped out of it as she felt the material pool at her feet. Thumbs hooked in the waistband of her knickers, drew them down and she, obligingly, stepped out of them.

In her mind's eye she conjured the lewd spectacle she must present. To how many pairs of eyes? Naked between the pearls at her throat and the thin strip of the garter belt at her waist. The black stockings held taut at mid-thigh emphasising her pale nudity.

"Hmm, good firm tits." A hand fondled her, fingers teased at the already bullet hard nipples, pressed them back into the surrounding aureolae only to let them spring back when released.

The hands stroked over her torso, descending to her midriff, fingers poking into her navel, stroking the fleece on her pubic mount. "Firm belly too. Must work hard to keep in shape."

"Nice fleshy bum, too," leather man's gruff whisper added, "firm though - no flab," and the fondling inspection of her posteriors ended in a light slap that rippled her buttock flesh.

They were discussing and inspecting her like some beast at a cattle show. Jayne felt her cheeks colour up. It was humiliation beyond her experience but beneath it all she felt a perverse excitement.

So the inspection and commentary continued. Hands stroked and pinched and probed. Her buttocks were parted, a wet finger sought and tickled at her crinkled anus. There were definitely two of them now but Jayne felt strangely aware of a third presence. Male or female she couldn't tell. She couldn't even be sure she had heard them or felt their touch. She simply felt the presence.

"On your knees," the rasped whisper ordered and a hand between her shoulder blades forced her down until she was kneeling, dog-like, on all fours.

"Oil her." The muffled, indistinct voice came from way behind her. "It will sting more."

A moment passed then Jayne felt cool liquid trickle over her lower back, forming a pool at her coccyx, dribbling along the cleft between her bum-cheeks. Firm hands, cupping the richly fleshed hemispheres, spread the oil over her buttocks and upper thighs. Those same hands spread her cheeks, liberally oiling the channel between, working the viscous stuff into her anus.

A leather strap slapped hard on her left bum-cheek, curling to embrace her flank. The first impact was a stinging shock making Jayne throw back her head and howl, wolflike, into the surrounding darkness. The leather slapped wetly over each bumcheek in turn - left and right, left and right - punishing the full roundness. Then it descended to sting the tender flesh where the ripe lobes of buttock met the ivory skin of upper thigh. Jayne wriggled and squirmed under the impact of each blow, yelling lustily with pain as her tortured fesses grew hotter and hotter.

Then they were finished. Jayne, in the silence, was acutely aware of her glowing cheeks as they throbbed painfully. Hands parted her buttocks and more oil was poured into the channel. Fingers worked it into the tight anal hole. Then she felt the solid flesh of an erect penis laid in the chasm between her parted buttocks, feeling it work up and down there. The tip touched against the puckered and slickly oiled porch of her rectum.

'My god, he's going to bugger me!' Half in fright and half in lascivious anticipation.

Slowly, steadily, the hardness was pressed into the tiny, tight-muscled aperture. Gradually she opened, swallowing it inside her. She screwed her eyes under the blindfold and set her teeth against the pain as the swollen head and half of the shaft penetrated her. Firm hands held her hips, pulling her back until she felt a flat belly against her throbbing fesses. He was in her, the thickness of him distending her rectal muscles as pleasure replaced pain.

She felt the lightest touch against her lips, a caress of velvet flesh that left a trail of moisture. The pressure became more insistent and she parted her lips to allow a stiffly erect penis to enter. It glided between her lips, over her tongue, forcing her jaws apart until the tip lodged in her throat.

Like a litany in her mind she told herself what was being done to her in the crudest terms she could command.

'He's buggering me. He's fucking my arse. I can feel him, so huge, working in and out of my rectum. I can feel him stretching me. His hands are in my cunt now, opening me. He's spreading my slime over my belly, over my tits. He's squeezing my tits, milking them as his big fat cock screws my arse. There's another fat cock in my mouth - fucking my mouth. They'll come soon and fill my arsehole and my mouth with their cream.'

She conjured mind pictures for herself - of her kneeling, her swollen bum in the air while a hard bodied, naked man rammed his thick tool into her distended bumhole, of his equally well endowed and naked partner burying his prick in her mouth.

Great waves of pleasure washed over her. She felt the penis in her mouth throb and seem to swell as gushes of seed hit the back of her throat. She swallowed it down automatically, gagging and choking as the weapon that was violating her rear end, as if with an independent animus, throbbed and poured gooey cream into her rectum.

In the brief silence that followed Jayne thought she heard a door waft open and click, almost imperceptibly, shut. A hand under her shoulder eased her upright until she was half kneeling, half sitting on her haunches. Without warning the blindfold was whipped away and Jayne blinked, half blind in the glaring light that suddenly burst on her retina.

As her vision cleared and she became used to the intense, white light, she saw the leather man standing in front of her. He was naked, his slim, hard body hairless and pale. His left hand caressed and cradled his erect penis that jutted from his groin, thick and long and ridged with veins. Jayne thought dimly, 'So there were three.'

"Take it, wank it," the low whisper commanded.

Jayne reached out with both hands. One cupped his scrotum, testing the weight of the eggs within and squeezing gently at the velvet sac. With the other she grasped the shaft and began to wank it firmly, squeezing the base at each stroke then firmly caressing from root to tip and back. Gradually she increased the vigour of the treatment until she detected a telltale twitching against the palm of her hand. She squeezed hard with both hands directing the eye of the penis at herself and wanked even harder. Instantly a hot, white jet of cream spewed at her, splashing over her nose and into her hair. Others followed, seeming to cover her face, shoulders and tits until the deflated instrument twitched its last.

Leather man tossed Jayne her discarded panties from the floor.

"Stand up and wipe yourself."

She got to her feet and used the scrap of lace edged silk to wipe the sticky effusion from her body. Standing, she became conscious of a cool stream of jism that oozed from her bumhole to trickle over her thighs down to the tops of her stockings.

Jayne had an opportunity to take stock of her surroundings. She seemed to be standing in the middle of a brightly lit and spacious dance studio. The walls were entirely composed of mirrors. Wherever she looked the lewdly naked image of herself was reflected back, and beyond that image still other reflections of her naked self, from different angles as if in a fantastic, bawdy kaleidoscope. To one side stood a wide bed covered with a single white satin sheet. There seemed to be no doors.

Also now, she could see who else was in the room with her. There were just two men. Leather man, of course, and beyond him a second man. He was shorter and more heavily built - built like a bull in fact. His close cropped head was set on powerful shoulders which merged into a muscular barrel chest. Thick legs supported his torso and at his core the thick, flaccid snake of his penis dangled. He was heavily tattooed. An eagle adorned his chest, a snake in gaudy reds and blues twined about his shoulders and encircled his neck. Even the shaft of his penis was decorated, with the image of a long stemmed rose in bud.

"Lie on the bed. On your back." The gruffly whispered command came from the leather man.

Jayne kicked off her shoes and swung her legs onto the bed, feeling the cool satin slippery against her skin. She propped her head on a couple of pillows and lay, supine, as she had been told.

The two men worked quickly. Leather man bound her wrists together with silky cords. Stretching them above her head he fastened them to the bedhead. The tattooed man parted her legs, spreading them wide and fastened her ankles to the two corner posts at the foot of the bed.

The girl appeared from nowhere, gliding into the room from some concealed doorway. She was coal black and stark naked, her satin pelt gleaming with a dull lustre in the intense light. Her small, high set breasts rode perkily on her breast bone as she strode with the springy steps of a gazelle towards Jayne's reclining form.

She stood beside the bed looking Jayne full in the face with an intense, unwavering gaze. Lying there, helpless, unable to move a muscle, Jayne felt an overwhelming urge to reach out and touch the sweet, night black cones and to suckle at the stiff, dark teats. As if reading her thoughts the girl inclined herself, offering her left breast to Jayne's lips. Hungrily she sucked the flesh into her mouth, grazing the titbit with her teeth.

The girl stood upright again and with a light, effortless movement swung her slim frame onto the bed. She straddled Jayne's body, placing a slender thigh on either side of the recumbent girl's head.

Jayne knew what she must do. Her tongue probed deeply into the black girl's sex, her lips sucked eagerly at her juices as she clamped her womanhood to her mouth. Her nostrils full of the girl's musky scent Jayne mouthed her pussy avidly. Very soon she brought her to the threshold of release and, her whole body shuddering with the intensity of the feeling, the black girl poured down a torrent of honeyed dew over Jayne's lips, tongue and chin.

Recovering, the girl dismounted from Jayne's face and again stood at the bedside. The tattooed man handed her a glass flask containing a yellow liquid. Slowly she withdrew the stopper and poured a stream of cool, heavily perfumed oil over Jayne's breasts and belly, allowing it to flow over her body and to dribble onto the satin sheet. Handing the half empty flask back, she began slowly and luxuriously to spread the oil evenly over Jayne's body, massaging her until she was slickly oiled from shoulders to toes.

For a while Jayne, her head spinning from the outrageous lewdness of what was happening to her, revelled in the young woman's touch which soon threatened to bring her to a screaming pitch of desire. When the black girl had finished and stood back from the bed Jayne opened her eyes.

She saw now that a third man had joined the party. Like the girl he was black, black as night. His body too had been oiled and he shone under the lights. He had the frame of a professional body-builder. His ebony skin was pulled taut over well developed pectorals. His muscles rippled as he stood.

He climbed onto the bed and like the girl before him straddled Jayne's face presenting his half hard manhood to her lips. Jayne smelt the odour of excited male mingled with the sweetness of the perfumed oil. She opened her mouth letting him feed in the long, thick stalk of flesh. Desperately she sucked on him, working her tongue to coat him with the moisture of her mouth, feeling him grow in her.

As soon as he was fully erect he withdrew from her. Holding himself with one hand he wiped the ebony wand over her face to smear her eyelids and nose with her own saliva. Working downwards he poked at her armpits, rolling the crown over her sensitive, shaven skin. He placed the stiff, black snake between her breasts, gathering the titflesh about it, squeezing her against the hardness. He worked his organ in the slickly oiled channel, pummelling at the yielding flesh, thrusting in and out.

Releasing her bosom he glided his body over hers, oiled flesh slipping over oiled flesh until after what seemed to Jayne to be a lifetime of bliss he knelt between her legs, his probe presented to the threshold of her womanhood. With a jerk of his hips he was inside her, buried to the hilt, his groin mashing against her pubic bone. He started to work in her, thrilling her while Jayne mewled her satisfaction.

Through a haze of delight Jayne just glimpsed the tattooed man couple with the girl, plunging into her from behind as she bent over the bed beside her. Then she was distracted by the leather man who, heavily erect again, thrust his tool between her lips.

As if perfectly orchestrated the three men worked themselves to the point of eruption while climaxes rippled through Jayne's body. As if by some prearranged signal the black man withdrew from her suddenly and kneeling between her outstretched legs began to bring himself off by hand. His companions followed suit and almost in unison their agitated weapons erupted to lance gouts of creamy spend over Jayne's body. She felt as if she was being covered in a torrent of male seed as their spending splashed over her belly and breasts, coated her pubic thatch and trickled onto the sheet beneath her.

Working together they released her and brought her to her feet.

"Get in the shower and clean yourself up," rumbled leather man curtly as he parted two of the mirrored panels to reveal a bathroom.

Stiffly, the male effusions already drying to a crust on her skin, Jayne crossed the floor to the shower. She stripped off the remnants of her stockings. They were ruined, covered in semen and snagged by the bonds which had secured her to the bed. She discarded the garter belt and stepped naked under the shower.

The needles of hot, hot water felt good on her skin. She found soap and worked up a lather, coating herself in the rich foam. Carefully she washed the stains from herself, then repeated the soaping and rinsing to rid her skin of the clinging perfumed oil. She was ready to step from the shower and was looking for a towel when leather man motioned her to stay put. Instantly the water turned from hot to ice cold. Jayne howled with shock and endured shuddering as the icy jets played over her skin.

When it was over she was a shivering mass of goose-flesh, her nipples puckered and hard like doorstops. Leather man took her wrist and lead her, dripping wet, to the centre of the room. He tied her wrists together using a leather strap, fixing it to a hook which hung suspended from a sturdy length of rope. The muscular Negro operated a concealed switch and with a whirring of machinery the rope was wound up into the ceiling until Jayne was at full stretch, arms tensioned above her head, just able to stand flat-footed on the thickly covered floor.

Once more Jayne was confronted with a reflection of herself. Her ivory skin was now scrubbed clean of all pollution. Her full, rounded breasts were drawn taut, her midriff concave as her body was strained upward. The tattooed man stepped behind her. A flail of leather thongs, knotted at the ends, dangled carelessly in his grasp.

Surrounded by the images of her own nakedness she saw the leather thongs arc towards her, saw them slash across her buttocks. She felt the pain and saw the crimson patch erupt on her flesh. She squealed and threw back her head. Her breasts quivered as a shudder of anguish rippled through her.

Totally immersed in the experience, every one of her senses acutely alive, she watched and felt as the tattooed man whipped her vigorously. The flail bit at her flesh until her back, buttocks and tender upper thighs had turned bright red. Salt tears welled up in her eyes and trickled down her cheeks. She wept with an uninhibited intensity, her bosom heaving with sobs drawn from deep within her.

She was on the point of begging for mercy when, as if sensing that her limit had been reached, the tattooed man relented. Her bottom ached, glowing with a fiery heat. And the whipping had rekindled other fires. She knew she had to be damp down there between her thighs, knew her sex must be awash.

The Negro, his phallus again in a state of erection, seated himself on an upright chair just behind her. His knees just grazed the back of her thighs. The motor whirred again and Jayne found her arms being relaxed as the rope unwound from the ceiling. The Negro's hands parted her legs and guided her over his lap. Her open pussy was positioned just above his uprearing tool. Clasping her hips he drew her down, fixing her on his thickly stiff erection, down until he was fully inside her.

Jayne had begun to climax as soon as the Negro's flesh had penetrated her. She wriggled on him, squealing and yelling as her body thrilled to the feel of him, groaning at the last as the final throes of pleasure died away.

They unhooked her then but left her hands bound together by the leather strap. The black man, his organ still healthily erect, lay on his back and his two companions helped Jayne to mount him again. She gurgled with pleasure as once again he entered her and completed their coupling. In the mirror she saw the tattooed man crouch behind her, felt him part her bum cheeks and with a quiver felt him steadily penetrate her anus until he was fully lodged in her rectum.

Finally, the leather man stood before her and grasping her hair, fed his stiff, meaty rod between her lips and into her throat. So they used her, working themselves inside her until one by one they again spilled their seed, each one into his chosen orifice.

Jayne lay panting on the floor, jism leaking from her bum hole and her pussy, lost in a sexual daze. Leather man pulled her to her feet and released her hands. Once more the blindfold was clamped to her eyes and she stood for long moments in darkness.

A hand clasped her wrist and a gruff command, "Come along," was rasped at her. Naked, she was lead again along corridors and through doors. She felt the cold night air on her bare skin, felt rough pavement under her bare feet. A coat was draped around her and she was bundled into the car.

Lost in the afterglow of all that had happened she could not tell, or even care, how long they drove. The car stopped and abruptly she was pulled from her seat. Doors slammed and the car had disappeared even before, in her dazed state, she reached up to remove the blindfold.

Dawn was just breaking and the morning was chill. She pulled the thin coat about her and only then realised she was standing in the pebbled driveway that led to her own house. The stones cut at her feet as she stumbled to the front door. She fumbled for keys in the coat pocket and let herself in. Her one desire now was to tumble into a warm, soft bed and sleep for a week!

With a satisfied sigh she climbed the stairs and entered her bedroom. Suddenly the bedside light snapped on, dazzling her temporarily. When her vision cleared she was dumbstruck to see George, propped up on the pillows, the covers carelessly arranged over his obviously naked form. He smiled at her blandly and drew back the covers:

"Good morning, my dear. I am sure you have had a most entertaining time. Come to bed and tell me all about it"

# POOR ALISON

## I

Poor Alison! Her life seemed to be a continual round of disasters, both social and professional. In short she was one of life's victims. She played the game without fully understanding the rules and without any consciousness of the consequences which inevitably followed even a minor infringement of any of them.

Her main problem was men. She had an unerring knack of picking out the wrong ones. Usually they were married and even those who were not just using her for a brief extra-marital fling eventually went back to their wives. Even the rare few who were not already spoken for turned out to be mother-fixated and in a short time returned to their first, true love. Alison gave them all her best and in return enjoyed very little beyond bitter tears and humiliation.

In her business life too an unusually large share of setbacks attended her efforts. It wasn't the case that she lacked expertise in her chosen field, which was antiques and fine art. On the contrary, she was very knowledgeable. It was rather that she let her enthusiasm and her basically trusting nature seduce her into too many rash decisions. All too often a worthless canvas became, in her eyes, an undiscovered work by some notable and fashionable artist. Having committed her funds, a more careful examination of the piece would soon show the valued item in its truc colours as a worthless piece of junk. Every time Alison lost not only her money but a little more of her diminishing stock of self-esteem.

Wisely, Alison's father had provided for her support after his death by setting up a virtually impregnable trust fund which was managed conservatively by the family lawyers. Under no circumstances could Alison touch or borrow against this capital. Her father had also advanced her the money to set up her own small antiques business, the running of which usefully occupied a large portion of Alison's day. Prudently run, this shop could have been a financial success, rendering the provision of a trust fund superfluous. Alison's frequent unwise speculations, however, often brought her enterprise to the brink of failure, so her father's thoughtful provision was ever necessary.

So it was that on her father's death Alison found herself alone in the world apart from two sisters who had moved with their husbands to, effectively, the other ends of the earth. Financially she was well provided for and, in fact, at a superficial level did not lack for friends. Thanks, however, to life's way of dealing her the sort of experience which deeply saps the morale, she needed, but lacked, a deeper, moral counsellor who could help her pick herself up and rebuild her self-image after each reverse.

Over the years that I have known her - more than ten at the last count - I have come to fill the role of father confessor and solid counsellor which once, so obviously, had been filled by her father. After each one of life's reverses she would come to me and pour out her heart, regaling me with the sad tales of her latest boyfriend's return to his wife or of her latest speculation which had turned to dust. We would discuss what remedy we might apply to assuage her guilt and her feelings of inadequacy. It must be said that she usually knows better than I what will be required to fit a given situation. Then we pursue the remedy agreed upon and in most cases Alison is readied to fight another engagement in life's battle.

My first experience of Alison's problems and the first time that she enlisted my help came about some three months after she had moved in to the flat next door to mine. During those three months she had occasionally knocked at my door to borrow coffee, sugar and so on, we had met and chatted briefly on the landing and once I had helped her carry up a weighty package. We were typical neighbours, polite but not on intimate terms.

One evening, shortly after dinner, I was disturbed by an urgent knocking at the front door. I opened to find an extremely distressed Alison on my doorstep. Tears streamed down her slim, oval face which, being devoid of makeup, seemed even paler than usual. I have often remarked since that Alison has a face made for misery since, while she is under normal circumstances a very pretty girl, sadness lends an additional cast of mysterious beauty to her features. I noticed that the poor girl was trembling as she blurted,

"P-p-please can I c-come in? I'm so unhappy. C-can you help me?"

Of course, I ushered her in and made her sit down in the living room. I went away to get some coffee and by the time I got back she had controlled herself a little and dried her tears although her eyes were still quite red and puffy. So it was that Alison, perched on my sofa and sipping her coffee, related her tale of woe, which in its generalities would become all too familiar to me over the years.

In this case, it seems her latest attachment, Guy by name, had omitted to mention that he already had a wife. Things had progressed famously until, quite by accident, Alison had seen Guy and his wife together in the street. Angry confrontations had followed with the result that Guy, who was just after a bit of extra-marital relief, dropped my friend like the proverbial hot potato. All of which left poor Alison feeling wretched, humiliated and with a severely deflated ego.

I could see that she was again on the point of tears as she finished her narrative and so I quickly asked how she thought I might be able to help her.

"Well," she began, blowing her nose noisily into the handkerchief I had lent her to staunch her tears, "when Daddy was alive, if we - that is my sisters and I - if we were naughty or did something foolish, we got a spanking. It always made me feel better. It got rid of the guilt feelings, I suppose. Since Daddy isn't here any more, well, I was wondering if you might ..."

I was staggered - more by the candid way in which she had put her request than by anything else, I suppose. It was quite uncanny how fate had laid this charming opportunity before me since, as I freely admit, I am something of an enthusiast in the matter of administering punishment.

"Tell me, Alison," I asked, "what form did these spankings take?"

She replied readily and without a trace of diffidence.

"It really depended on the nature and gravity of the crime. You see, if we had been really naughty - stayed out past bedtime, not put in enough effort on homework - then we might get the cane. I even got the birch once! But if we had just been silly - overspent on pocket money, say - then we got a hand spanking or maybe with a leather paddle. I think today a paddling ought to be just the thing. Do you have one?"

Did I have one? The innocence of the question!

"Well - perhaps I could find something of that sort - and you would like me to spank you with it?" I hoped the excitement did not show too much in my voice.

Alison nodded her agreement and I left her to fetch the instrument in question. It was, as a matter of fact, a rather fine specimen, quite broad and thick but without losing the pliability essential in such devices. I went back into the room and sat down again, holding the paddle out for my intended victim to examine and approve.

"I'm sure that that will be just right. How do you want me?"

I had sensed already that Alison knew very well what she wanted and that I should refrain from introducing my own partialities into the situation. With just a little prompting the dear girl would of herself lead us to a mutually satisfactory outcome.

"Tell me, how did Daddy arrange things when he punished you?" I answered.

"Of course, then, everybody, Mummy and we three sisters, would be present to witness the punishment. The guilty party would have to undress - quite naked - to receive their punishment."

"Then that is how it shall be now. Take off your clothes."

Unhurriedly, but without the slightest trace of hesitation, Alison undressed herself. It was not a strip-tease, there was no element of tease about her actions. Rather, she so arranged her movements as to give me the best possible view of her charming frame as she gradually revealed herself.

Carefully, as she removed each garment, she folded it and placed it neatly on the coffee table. Soon she was naked but for her stockings and garter belt. She sat and, unhooking each nylon sheath, she drew it sensuously down her smooth legs, gathering the loose material in both hands as she rolled it down thigh and calf, drawing the ball of nylon at last from her foot and adding it to the small pile of discarded clothing on the table. The garter belt soon followed and she stood totally nude before me.

It was obvious that her father had made sure that Alison was well schooled in the practices of self-abasement. Automatically she placed her hands behind her head to offer me an unhindered view of her bare, pale flesh. Very slowly and with downcast eyes she began to turn around making sure to let me savour every inch of her body as she showed herself to me. I, for my part, frankly admired the charming spectacle that was so openly displayed for my delight.

In her nakedness Alison was a true pre-Raphaelite beauty. Flaming red hair tumbled over her shoulders and framed her sadly beautiful face. Her skin was the purest, milkiest white, like fine Meissen porcelain with just a light dusting of freckles at her chest and shoulders. The snowy whiteness was relieved by the red tuft that covered her pubis and the puckered coral of the nipples that capped the perfect cones of her sweet, small breasts.

As she turned I noted with some satisfaction that she had a fine bottom, well fleshed but firm. I was certainly going to enjoy punishing such a perfectly formed arse.

Eventually, when she had sensed that I had looked my fill, Alison stood still and lowered her arms to her sides with a rueful smile.

"Now we would have to confess our crime or tell over our shortcomings so that everyone could hear. But I think I have already bored you enough with tales of my silliness this evening. So shall we let that bit pass?"

I nodded my assent and she continued,

"Then we would have to ask for our punishment, so here goes. Since I have been so stupid, please would you spank me very hard on my bare backside. Please don't spare me. Let me really feel the paddle doing me good."

Against one wall there was a chaise longue with a fine curled back which I had often used on such occasions as these. I directed Alison to kneel on it, facing the back so she could stretch out across the back support and thus, by slightly arching her back push her bottom up into the ideal position to receive my attention. Without the need for further instruction she flattened her upper body against the soft velours and, legs slightly parted so the ripe ovoids of her buttocks were pushed apart, thrust her bottom upwards.

I went to work with the paddle on her opulent bum-flesh straight away, first warming her with a few deft flicks, then really pounding away as her flesh rippled under the impact. I realised that there was no need to gentle her along, here under my hand was a veritable habituee and so I worked her hard just as she had asked.

At first she made no sound, just marking the impact of each blow with a sharp intake of breath. Gradually though, as the blows and the pain intensified, she allowed herself to moan and cry out. I sensed, however, that this was as much to encourage me as to give vent to her feelings.

Very soon the milky flesh of her posteriors had taken on a fiery hue which contrasted deliciously with the rest of her body. I stopped to admire my handiwork and to marvel at her quivering flesh but she urged me on, begging me to continue as hard as possible.

So we continued until by an unspoken mutual agreement it was deemed that she had suffered sufficiently for her needs. I helped her to get to her feet and she, in a soft voice, completed the ritual by humbly thanking me for spanking her, intimating at the same time how much better she felt as a result.

Over the next several years this episode was repeated time and time again. Alison would appear on my doorstep greatly distressed. She would pour out her troubles and we would discuss an appropriate remedy which I would then administer. I found it quite remarkable how Alison always seemed able to touch upon exactly the remedy she required to suit every circumstance. In this I came to trust her judgement and self-knowledge implicitly and would never quibble over the degree of severity she herself demanded.

Of course, during all this time we became close friends - but let us be clear on this, nothing more than friends. We found much in common in our mutual love of the arts and fine art in particular. We spent long evenings looking over my small collection of lesser Victorian artists and Alison even contrived to enrich the collection from time to time. We often dined together and spent many happy evenings in each other's company. Eventually she moved to a more spacious flat but we continued to meet, albeit a little less regularly.

It was some four months since I had heard from Alison. This was an ominous sign since long silences often betokened a new involvement with a man and this was one of the longest silences yet. I ardently wished the poor girl well but any day now I expected a tearful visit, and I was proved right.

There she stood on my doorstep, the tears streaming down her cheeks, too mortified even to speak. I led her into the sitting room and tried to get her to sit down and calm herself but at first she could do no more than pace up and down, clenching and unclenching her fists. At last I got her to take a little brandy and by dint of soft words and coaxing got her seated in front of the fire.

For some time she just sat staring into the flames as great sobs from deep inside her shook her slender frame. More brandy was taken and eventually she was able to utter,

"He bloody left me ...the bastard left me!"

At least the floodgates were starting to open, so I coaxed some more and eventually, confession being good for the soul, her story poured out. The brandy was taking hold now and she became quite loquacious.

Certainly, as suspected, there had been a new man. Young, handsome and above all unmarried and with no other female in sight. All had been bliss for four months. He had moved in with her. What could have gone wrong?

"And then the bastard left me. Left me today," Alison snuffled. "But the worst of it was he left me for another man. He was queer, gay, bloody bent! And I wasted four months on him."

Again she dissolved into tears. I sat beside her and put a friendly arm about her shoulder, cuddling her quaking body to me in a vain effort to comfort her.

"But that's not the worst of it," she wailed through her tears. "I gave him presents too, you see. I gave him Daddy's cuff-links and his gold hunter. Oh, I'm such a fool!"

I was forced to agree with her that this was probably the worst mess she had ever made for herself. For a while she continued to alternately sob and rail against the latest man who had betrayed her while I gently cuddled her to me. She calmed down considerably when I pointed out that her lover would most likely not hold onto the presents she had, as now seemed the case, forced on him but would probably be persuaded to hand them back if I visited him.

Gradually she calmed down and the tears were eventually staunched. Slowly she sipped more brandy and apart from the sadness in her eyes she came to look more like herself.

"Now the crying's over," she began, "I suppose I should take my medicine and pay for my stupidity."

"Do you think you are in a fit state?" I asked uncertainly. "You are still quite overwrought. Would it not be better to rest first, get a good night's sleep?"

"No. No, I think I will be a lot better for receiving my due dose right now. Anyway I wouldn't sleep without it."

"Well, you know best what will help you now," I acquiesced. "Do you have something in mind?"

"Since, as we agree, this is probably the worst mess I've made, the punishment needs to be something pretty exacting. Really painful and er... quite prolonged and well... humiliating too."

I simply nodded, knowing that she already knew clearly what was wanted and would tell me in her own time.

"First of all you will have to give me a sound and thorough beating on my naked body. I mean thorough: bottom, back, legs. Really stripe me - draw blood if necessary. You have quite a heavy whip - a punishment cat? Use that."

I called the instrument in question to mind; a heavy and vicious thing, a cat o' nine tails made of thick leather thongs. I shuddered involuntarily at the thought of it biting at poor Alison's soft, white flesh. But she had chosen and there would be no gainsaying her.

"If that is what you want, OK," I agreed reluctantly, "but you won't be in a fit state to go home alone afterwards. Better to stay with me for a few days until you recover."

She smiled quietly at that and continued,

"Dear Tony, that's just what I had in mind. In fact that's to be part of the punishment too - the humiliation part. I think I should stay with you as your servant - wait upon you, do your washing or any menial thing you can think of. Of course, you must act the master! Make me dress, or undress, to please you and punish me if I fail to please."

I said that I understood and went off to fetch the whip and some other necessary items for when we had finished. When I returned Alison had already started to undress and was naked to the waist. She was soon quite naked and stood in front of me eyeing the whip as I let the leather thongs slip idly between my fingers. I indicated that she should take up her usual position on the chaise longue, which she did. I paused to admire her bottom which was still a delight after years of intimate acquaintance, the smooth hemispheres of firm muscle quivering slightly in anticipation of the punishment to come.

I allowed her to brace herself, fingers digging into the soft padding as she lay prone and defenceless. She nodded slightly to indicate that she was ready and I began.

Lightly at first, just enough to bring colour to her cheeks, but then with increasing intensity, I worked the lash over the satin smooth mounds of her bottom. Alison's habitual stoical silence under punishment was soon abandoned and she yelped lustily as the leather thongs clasped her in their stinging embrace. Her bottom soon coloured up to a rich carmine and I shifted my focus, first to the backs of her thighs, then with her lower limbs satisfyingly reddened, up to her back and shoulders.

I plied the whip with great deliberation allowing my victim to mark each bitter cut of the leather on her yielding flesh and then to fully savour the lingering pain. The staccato slap of the leather thongs on the glowing flesh counterpointed her agonised squeals but she did not flinch. Bravely she clung to the chaise while fingers and toes dug hard into the cushions as if to a raft in a stormy sea. Her face contorted in a grimace of agony but no tears came - she had already cried herself dry!

At last, after the poor girl had endured an agonising hour of torment and her flesh had taken on a ripe plum hue, I put up the whip. A mass of weals criss-crossed her back and similar disfigurements ridged her bottom and thighs. Her breath came in shallow draughts and her yelps of pain had become mere hoarse whispers. Gently I stroked her hair.

"Alison, if I persist now I will draw blood. This is enough now."

"No, carry on. You must finish me thoroughly."

Again I took up the whip and again laid it across her. Soon, I knew, ruby droplets would have appeared on her tortured flesh. I knew then that for her own good I must, at the last, gainsay her. Now I knew she must suffer no more and I tossed the whip aside. She had endured bravely but enough is enough. Gently I bathed her wounds and used the antiseptic ointments I had set ready on the table before our ritual had begun.

As would be expected, she was exhausted by her ordeal. I fed her a little more brandy and carried her to my guest bedroom. She was asleep by the time I kissed her gently on the cheek and she continued thus late into the next afternoon.

I nursed her for some days, cleaning and dressing her wounds, feeding her and making sure that she rested. Soon she recovered her old vitality and the lacerations on her sweet flesh began to heal. Then, recovered, she entered on the second part of her punishment - to serve and humbly obey me in the character of a servant.

She entered gladly into this role and I needed to play the master very little. It seemed that no task was beneath her and she waited on me hand and foot. Of course, more for the sake of form than anything else, I would chastise her, but even that seemed superfluous, so diligent was she in humbling herself to serve me.

One morning, maybe two weeks after her ordeal, she brought me my breakfast in bed as usual. As I ate she perched on my bed beside me, rubbing herself against me in a companionable sort of way. She was wearing an old pyjama jacket of mine which just about covered her bottom but left her shapely legs temptingly bare.

"I've decided what will be best for me in the future," she began archly.

With a mouthful of egg, I could only wait for the revelation.

"I need to find a man who loves me enough to really take me in hand," she went on, "to guide me and chastise me. Then I need to place myself wholly under his control - just love him and serve him."

I wholly missed the meaningful look she was sending my way.

"Tony," she began again after a few seconds of silence, "in all these years haven't you ever wanted to sleep with me?"

I swallowed hard, clearing my mouth of the last of my breakfast. What a question!

"My dear Alison," I began, "I would have had to have been made of stone not to want to go to bed with you. But we are friends and I believe our rather special friendship is very important to you. If we were to become er ... lovers, then we would complicate and possibly destroy the friendship we have. In other words, I would not be able to help you in the way I have over these years. So, I've made it a rule to control my desires where our friendship is concerned."

Alison hugged me and treated me to a smacking kiss on the cheek.

"What a darling man you are! Yes, you are a very special friend. So special that I think I must arrange something very special for you to reward these years of devotion. Just you wait and see if I don't."

And there, with an enigmatic smile, she let the matter, whatever it was, lie.


II


Alison, as things worked out, was exactly as good as her word.

Another couple of weeks passed and she was soon completely recovered from her ordeal under the lash of the cat. Gradually she began to combine her self-imposed penance of serving me with visits to her shop to keep her antiques business ticking over. Soon enough she was back full time at the shop and busily looking after me in the evenings and at the weekends. At last she seemed to be completely over her recent bad experience with yet another worthless man.

She still, however, showed no sign of wanting to get back to her own flat. Occasionally she would pop back to retrieve some more clothes or some vital piece of culinary equipment but that was all. Effectively she had moved into my guest bedroom and it seemed as if she planned to take up residence for good.

My birthday came around and Alison announced that we should have a little dinner party to celebrate. She would cook something special for the occasion. So she set to and spent several hours in my tiny kitchen from which I was effectively and practically barred.

I became engrossed in one of the books which I had received as presents and was a little annoyed to be disturbed by a ringing at the doorbell just before I expected that we should sit down to eat.

I was astonished, on opening the door, to be confronted by a most fetching young woman - tall, well built and attractively sun tanned. A brilliant smile, full lipped and teeth-flashing, lit up her whole face as she noticed my total, flabbergasted surprise.

"Hi. You must be Tony. I'm Carole - I'm for your birthday. I guess Alison kept me for a surprise."

Her strong Australian accent was not unpleasant. Remembering my manners at last, I took the hand she held out to me to shake and welcomed her in.

She wore a thick sweater against the chill of the autumn evening and a brief mini-skirt that showed off her long sun-tanned legs to perfection. I had plenty of opportunity to enjoy the sight of those very shapely legs as she sat on my sofa, crossing them sinuously, and accepted the drink I offered her.

Alison popped her head around the kitchen door for a second to welcome her friend and went right back to her pots and pans. So I was left to entertain our unexpected but certainly not unwelcome guest for some time while Alison bustled about preparing for dinner. And who would not relish the thought of spending an idle hour chatting and flirting - oh yes, Carole flirted openly from the start - with an attractive, subtly perfumed and attractively animated young woman like Carole.

I enjoyed her forthright manner of speaking and was attracted by her frankness in putting forth her opinions which is so typical of her nation. In short we got on famously and were soon more like friends of long acquaintance than the virtual strangers which in fact we were.

In the course of our chat I found out that Carole was indeed from Australia, Sydney in fact, and like many of her compatriots she was taking some time out to visit the 'Old Country' and fitting in some trips around Europe. She had been helping Alison in the shop for a couple of months now and had looked after things when Alison took her little holiday under my care.

At last dinner was served, and by this time I was frankly ravenous. Alison dimmed the lights to a romantic candle assisted gloom and the three of us sat down to do justice to the very fine meal she had prepared. I was glad to see that her parents had looked well to her domestic education as well as ensuring that she was properly disciplined.

The dining nook in my flat was just that, a small area for bachelor dinners or entertaining tête-à-tête. With three of us around the table, myself flanked by my two charming companions, it was an intimate gathering marked by the companionable closeness of the participants. All through the meal Carole continued to flirt quite outrageously and, not inexperienced though I am, I felt myself blushing on occasions. From time to time too, her hand would firmly grasp and caress my thigh while occasionally I would feel bare toes brushing against my ankles.

By the end of the meal I was becoming quite excited by the overt attention I was receiving from our guest. Alison for her part seemed mildly amused and, if anything, encouraged her friend to some of her wilder excesses. I pushed my chair back from the table and suggested that a little brandy with coffee might not come amiss. Carole slipped to the floor so that she was kneeling between my outstretched legs and looked up with an arch grin and a twinkle in her eyes.

"I thought you might like some more dessert first!"

Without waiting for a response, which the condition of my clothing made superfluous, she began to loosen my belt and to draw trousers and pants together down my legs. Obligingly, I lifted my bottom so she could ease my clothes down and over my already tumescent manhood. She was most expert and had dexterously removed all my lower garments in a few seconds, leaving me bared below the waist with my full erection pointing aggressively at the ceiling.

"I meant what I said when I arrived, Tony. I'm for your birthday. Your special present from Alison - get it?" As she spoke she grasped my manhood, fondling it gently. The rod of tensed flesh jerked slightly under her touch conveying my understanding.

She continued to run her hands lightly over my stiffly erect flesh. She reached out a soft hand to cup the loose skin of my scrotum, weighing the contents. She murmured approval as she inspected the twitching flesh rod minutely.

"Hmm, he's very, very nice. We are both going to enjoy this immensely," she finally remarked with another mouthful of a smile.

Flicking a few stray strands of her short, fair hair from her face she bent her head and teasingly began to run her tongue over my penis. Tantalisingly she trailed her mouth over my inner thighs, over my belly, approaching but never quite reaching my uprearing sex. Lightly, her small, sharp teeth nipped at the skin of my tummy. Then she was off again, making a trail of dampness over my sensitized skin.

Soon enough she drew back and began again to give some attention to my cock which now strained upwards in a most agitated state. Steadying my organ with one hand at the base, she put out her tongue and tentatively licked at the tip. As if acquiring the taste, she licked slowly over the velvety smooth crown. She drew back the foreskin to expose the glans and treated the whole dome to a lavish bath of her saliva. Soon she was tonguing wetly over the entire, uprearing shaft of swollen meat, little growls of pleasure gurgling softly in her throat.

I just lay back and revelled in the electric sensations that invaded me entirely. I have an average amount of self-control but was sure that I couldn't last much longer - so I just gave myself to the moment and relaxed.

Now her lips were over the crown, her tongue flicking at the tip of my straining engine. Her mouth worked down the shaft to draw more and more of me into the velvet moist cavern. Teeth and tongue worked on me still and at last I found myself lodged wholly between her jaws, throat deep. Gently, agonizingly slowly, she released and recaptured my hardness, nodding her head up and down as the crown collided with the roof of her mouth. I couldn't hold on much longer. My fingers grasped the arm of my chair, the knuckles white as the delicious sexual tensions built in me.

With a soft 'plop' Carole released me and hunkered back on her thighs. The tension in me relaxed and I opened my eyes. Quickly, grasping the hem, she drew the heavy sweater over her head and was naked to the waist. Her massy, bra-less breasts flopped down, released from confinement, the delightfully soft sacs of ripe, white flesh contrasting with the deep tan of the rest of her upper body. Quite obviously not a topless sunbather.

Her rosy red nipples were already engorged with passion, standing stiff on the snowy mounds like India rubbers. She cupped her bosom, one hand under each generous globe, raising them up as if offering them to me. Then, leaning forward, she wrapped the soft, satin smooth flesh around my hot, wetly slick male hardness, squeezing it between her breasts. With painful slowness she worked her titties up and down my straining tool, the tip emerging between the tit-flesh and threatening to impale her chin. Very soon her bosom was smeared with her own saliva melded with the oily lubricant that now oozed from my severely agitated maleness. Once again I was on the verge of spending and my anxious weapon throbbed urgently.

Sensing the imminence of my need, Carole released me from my comfortable imprisonment between her breasts and quickly engulfed me again in her mouth, sliding my rod between her lips until the crown lodged in her throat. My cream boiled in me and there was to be no more holding back. My insides convulsed violently as my spending pumped violently from me, gushing a creamy effusion to fill Carole's mouth. She swallowed every drop and with a parting lick released my already waning tool. She leaned back on her haunches with a smile and a satisfied sigh.

"Delicious. Just delicious."

But by no means was that the end of things. Carole got to her feet and, hiking the mini-skirt over her finely contoured thighs, straddled my legs and settled herself facing me, on my lap. A brief glimpse of the fair bush on her mons sufficed to show me that the dear girl had not bothered with underwear at all. Expertly her fingers worked at my buttons and my shirt was removed.

She leaned forward on me, her cool breast flesh spreading against my chest and gave me a deep, tongue sucking kiss. She thrust her tits at me then, inviting my attention. I took an opulent fleshy tear-drop in each hand, feeling the pleasing weight, enjoying the warm smoothness of the skin on my palms. Gently I massaged the two firm globes, feeling the elasticity of the pliant gourds.

"Hmmm! Squeeze them hard. Make me squeal," Carole invited throatily.

I tightened my grip at her urging, kneading and squeezing the rich flesh which overflowed my fingers as I grasped tighter and tighter. With each spasm of pain Carole moaned low in her throat and the moan subtly resolved itself into a groan of pleasure.

My fingers twisted the tortured flesh of her bosom drawing the massy fruit into cones as I took her rubbery nipples between finger and thumb, squeezing unmercifully.

Carole writhed under my hands, urging me on. "Oooh, that's good! Harder, squeeze harder. Aaah, mmm."

I raised her left breast to my lips, sucking the engorged nipple between my lips, licking over the bud and the surrounding aureola.

"Yess! Bite them! Bite them! Hurt me!"

Carole's sharp finger nails fastened to my shoulders, urging me to do as she begged.

I framed my teeth about the rubbery bud and sucked hard to draw it firmly into my mouth grazing the sensitive flesh. Carole sighed and moaned and squealed her approval but continued to mutter, "Harder. Bite me, please!"

Taking each sweet bud in turn I chewed on her nipples and the surrounding flesh as her nails raked my flesh. She was in a real frenzy now, alternately howling in pain and sighing with pleasure. Tears of pain - or was it ecstasy? - flowed copiously down her cheeks. I left her breasts alone for a moment to lap at the salty stream.

My manhood had by this time regained some of its former vigour and was probing like a stiffened finger at Carole's bare backside as she wriggled excitedly on my lap. Deftly she fished between my legs and catching the importunate fellow by the root fixed him effortlessly in her well lubricated sex.

I reached behind her and cupped her buttocks as they rose and fell over my lap. I drew the plump cheeks apart and probed the deep furrow between, seeking and finding her anus. I poked at the little crinkled orifice and then wiggled an index finger into the tight cavity, prompting an 'Mmmm!' of approval from my partner.

Urgently she whispered in my ear as she rode my erection with deep thrusts of her hips, "Bite my tits! Hurt me! Do it! Do it!"

So I browsed on the abundance of her tit-flesh. Starting at the base and nipping with my teeth then drawing gobbets of the yielding flesh into my mouth and biting hard. To an accompaniment of her pained yells and pleasured sighs I covered the snowy mounds in a mass of love-bites.

Allowing Carole's bosom a brief respite while I worked my teeth at her neck and shoulders I caught a glimpse of Alison, who had been quite forgotten until now. She too was entering into the spirit of the occasion. Her skirt was hiked up above her waist, her panties dangled limply from one ankle and a heavy silver salt cellar was doing duty in her drooling fanny. She was completely oblivious to anything else, urging herself to greater and greater excitements with the thick silver tube.

I returned my attention to Carole who clung to me still, talons fixed in my shoulders while the muscles of her sex clasped at my manhood as a succession of tiny thrills, building to her ultimate climax, rocked her body. I continued to chew on her wonderfully elastic flesh as she gasped and moaned, writhing against me. Then, inevitably, a quaking orgasm overwhelmed her and with a deep throated groan of release she hugged me to her and bit hard on my shoulder.

I, for my part, had held back until now with some difficulty and with relief gave up the struggle, washing her love tube with liberal gushes of my overheated sexcrement.

Panting, Carole collapsed against me, mingling the sweat that filmed our bodies and murmured,

"Great! Bloody great."

My new friend's recuperative powers were truly remarkable. In a few moments she was on her feet again, fumbling with the fastenings of the miniskirt and tossing it to one side.

"Now you can smack my bottom! Ali says you're very good. You can let me have it really hard. No love pats, right?"

She turned on her heels, heading for the bedroom, letting me have a good look at her extravagantly fine bottom. The ripely jiggling hillocks of resilient flesh, creamy white against the golden tan of her back and legs, were just asking for a firm tawsing. My interest kindled anew, I followed. Alison, who had now removed all her clothing, followed too.

I placed a couple of pillows at the foot of the bed to support my victim's hips and push her bottom up and outwards. Carole, in a matter of fact way, draped herself over them, parting her legs slightly to present me with her heavy buttocks spread in a broad target. I ran my hand over the warmly silken skin appreciatively, plumping the rich fatness of her arse and finishing by pinching her hard on the right cheek. She let out a little 'Oh!' almost in mock surprise as the mark of my fingers quickly faded from the whiteness.

Alison seemed to have appointed herself as my assistant and had fetched a tawse from my collection in the wardrobe. It was an old friend, well used but still supple, having lost the irritating stiffness of a new instrument.

So, taking Carole at her word, I began to whack her bottom lustily with the tawse. Her flesh reddened up nicely and the widely spread bum cheeks quivered attractively as the leather pummelled them. I took care to ensure that no area of the target was neglected, thoroughly pasting the full rondures of the massy hemispheres but also attending to her upper thighs and flanks. Carole gave every indication of enjoyment, squealing with each fresh impact while her face contorted with pain but then groaning with pleasure between each stroke.

I paused briefly to enjoy the heat from her glowing fesses, passing my palm over the quivering, stinging mass. Carole, impatiently, urged me on, demanding more and harder.

The excitement of all this activity communicated itself to my manhood which again rose up to demand a share of attention. The stiff rod of flesh swayed maniacally beneath my groin as I exerted myself on Carole's bottom. I had placed a long cheval glass by the bed so that Carole could get a good view of me working on her bottom and now, by the same means, she could observe my own excited state.

"Fuck me in the arse." she begged, her bottom twitching from the last stroke of the tawse. "Come on now, stick it up my bumhole!"

Alison, still in her role of assistant, stood ready with a pot of lubricant she had fetched in anticipation of this outcome. She applied a generous portion to my uprearing manhood. Then, when I was properly prepared, she seized her friend's bumcheeks, parting them to reveal the puckered entrance to Carole's rectum. I fixed the head in the tight orifice which yielded easily to this intrusion, then without holding back, ploughed my full length into Carole's back passage. She yelped at the initial shock then pleasure took over and she wriggled against me to deepen the penetration.

Clasping her hips I began to work in her, grinding my belly against her still ruddy bumcheeks as I fucked her with a slight rotating motion. Gradually I increased the vigour and power of my thrusts almost burying the poor girl in the bed covers.

I slipped my rod from her rectum and glided it easily into her sex without spoiling the rhythm of our motions. I reached under her, grasped her breast and squeezed, using her mammaries to lever myself deeper inside her. Carole's cunt walls clasped my staff as if approving the action.

So we worked together as climaxes rippled through Carole's body and I too approached another moment of blissful release. Carole, sensing the approaching deluge, grunted through clenched teeth,

"In my arse. Come in my arse."

How could I resist? Again I buried myself in her bumhole, feeling the rectal walls clasp at me. A few more strokes and it was time. Hot creamy jism burst from me to wash the tightness of Carole's rectum as my tool pumped crazily inside her.

I withdrew my wilting manhood and climbed onto the bed levelling my groin with Carole's face. She took the well used flesh and rubbed it over her face to smear herself with the sticky mixture of her own juices and my salty spend before popping it into her mouth to lick it sparkling clean.

Exhausted, I sprawled on the bed with a couple of pillows supporting my head and shoulders. Carole, on the other hand, was by no means finished and she and Alison were soon embraced in a frenzied 'soixante-neuf'. I watched entranced as the two girls ran the gamut of Sapphic pleasure. The last thing I remember before drifting of to a well earned sleep was the sight of the Junoesque Carole, now sporting a huge dildo strapped at her groin, serving the slender Alison who was kneeling on all fours and groaning with lust.

Through the night I slept deeply, coming almost awake from time to time to sense myself surrounded by warm, comforting female flesh. When daylight finally clawed its way beneath my eyelids and I dragged myself awake a soft female hand was clasping my already swollen maleness. The hand belonged to Alison who was sleeping soundly beside me, her red hair spread on the pillow like Burne-Jones Ophelia.

Hell! Rules were made to be broken and maybe our friendship was due to move on to something more. I rolled over and kissed her mouth. Then more kisses followed over her neck, her shoulders. I tasted her breasts, licking at her nipples which were passive and relaxed in sleep. Soon she awoke and returned my attentions as her hand again sought and found my manhood.

A smile of sweet contentment lit her face as she opened herself to me, parting her thighs to receive me as she lay beneath me. I entered her smoothly, pushing my swollen manhood into the moistly clasping cavern of her sex. She clung to me while I worked inside her, circling my waist with her slender legs and clasping me to her.

The pace of our union quickened and Alison groaned and sighed as little ripples of excitement coursed through her body. She climaxed deliriously, clamping her nails into my flesh and I too found my release, jetting my creamy tribute deep inside her.

In that moment of pure time-stopping bliss, Alison's words as she curled next to me, wearing my old pyjamas came back to me. Maybe she had found the right man at last.


After that, events just seemed to follow a natural progression. Of course we had to move from the flat. It was just too small for the three of us. Oh yes, Carole stayed too.

Alison still gets into messes from time to time. Nothing like as serious before, however, our stable home life sees to that. Anyway she has a big sister and a big brother to keep her on the straight and narrow. Besides, when she errs there are still the good old remedies to be vigorously applied.

Curled in the warmth beneath the heavy quilt, Jacqueline journeyed towards wakefulness. She stirred and put forth a tentative hand to test the space formerly occupied by her lover. The sheets were cold, showing that he had been gone for some hours. There was no pressing reason to get up. Jacqueline burrowed under the covers and drowsed in her nest.

Eventually, further oblivion became impossible. Her mind teemed with thoughts, with images of the night before. She was definitively awake. With a supreme effort she forced her head above the quilt, up up into the bright daylight. She opened her eyes and at once screwed them closed again as the brightness jarred on her vision. Gradually she eased the lids apart again, beginning slowly to acclimatise herself to the sunlight which, although filtered by the curtains, lit her bedroom with a harsh and glaring effect.

Lazily she continued to lie there, flat on her back, just staring at the ceiling and letting her mind idle, not engaged by any particular thought. Another act of will and she pushed the quilt from her and swung her legs over the side of the bed, planting her feet on the floor.

She picked up a silk robe and swung it about her shoulders. Fastening it tightly about her with a matching silken sash she padded on bare feet to the kitchen. She made coffee and sat at breakfast, picking listlessly at a croissant left over from yesterday.

Now she had to face the question which had become her daily challenge. How was she to spend the day?

How should she fill the hours until Henri was with her again? Assuming that tonight he would have the time to visit her. Assuming that he did not have some other pressing engagement involving his wife, his family or his business. Jacqueline pondered her options while she sipped the hot milky coffee and chewed at the rubbery flesh of the stale croissant.

Lunch would be nice. Yes, lunch in a pleasant, discreet restaurant where the service is attentive. Lunch with a friend, some gossip ... But since she had known Henri Jacqueline had gradually lost touch with her girl-friends. Now she could not think of anyone she might just call up on the off-chance and invite to lunch. It must have been more than six months since she last saw Chloe, and she had been her closest friend. And before that? Well ...

Naturally, there were no boy-friends. There had been Edouard at the start. Yes, she had even been engaged to Edouard. But then the affaire with Henri had begun and gradually it had taken over her life, leaving no place for anyone else.

So it would have to be lunch alone.

Jacqueline called to mind the perfect restaurant; quiet, discreet, a place where a woman dining alone would pass unremarked, where the staff could still be relied upon to cosset a guest, even if she were unescorted.

And afterwards? Perhaps a little shopping. Yes, a visit to two or three favourite boutiques or an amble through the Galleries Lafayette could always be relied upon to pass a few hours pleasantly enough. Henri, quite naturally, provided his mistress with plenty of clothes and jewellery too. Indeed recently he would become quite upset if Jacqueline should buy anything for herself without his express permission. It was not that he was mean; quite the contrary. It was, as he explained, that he wished to be sure that her appearance would please him and so she should be sure to consult him first. 'Anyway,' Jacqueline thought, 'it's still nice to look.'

So the little programme she had mapped out for herself would fill up the empty hours of the day and bring her back to the apartment ready for five o'clock. She must be back for five because that was when Henri would telephone. If he telephoned. Of course, he might call later or just turn up unannounced and let himself in. But if he chose to telephone at five o'clock it would please him to find Jacqueline in and waiting for his call.

Her breakfast finished and her plans laid for the day, Jacqueline busied herself with her toilet. Every morning she carried out this ritual punctiliously; to please herself certainly, for what woman does not enjoy tending to her own appearance, but above all the ritual was followed to please Henri. One day she had suffered an hour long lecture on the subject because Henri had appeared unannounced around midday to take her to the races and had found her lounging in jeans, her hair uncombed and her face devoid of makeup. His views, of course, had been most reasonable, as were all of the things he required of his mistress, and the young woman, eager to please him, made sure in the future that she was always properly prepared to receive him.

She drew a steaming bath, adding aromatic oils to cleanse and soften her skin and relaxed in the hot, sweetly perfumed water. She soaped herself well, noticing the bruise at the base of her breast where, the night before,

Henri had bitten her at the height of his passion. She lapsed into a daydream again, recalling the events of the previous evening.

Certainly Henri was a perfect lover - vigorous and full of energy and invention. As if by intuition he knew when and where to caress, to squeeze, to lick or to bite in order to lift Jacqueline to the heights of bliss. His hard, lean body covered her, moulding to her softer, yielding flesh. His thick, proud manhood probed her, thrilling her to the core. How could she not desire him and want him throughout her every waking moment?

The water was cooling now and Jacqueline, waking from her reverie, climbed out of the bath. She towelled herself dry vigorously, the chafing of the coarse towel making her skin glow. Then, properly dried, she dusted herself liberally with perfumed talc, the fine particles reaching her nose, making her sneeze.

Finished in the bathroom, she strode naked to the bedroom. She interrupted her preparations to rearrange the dishevelled bed and then in a leisurely and thoughtful manner selected her outfit for the day.

Before dressing she perfumed herself thoroughly, using one of Henri's favourite fragrances. She applied the sweet essence to the cleavage between her full breasts, then raised the heavy, fleshy globes to smear the undersides. She applied some to her abdomen, a little between her legs and finally along the dark furrow that separated her buttocks.

She drew black nylon stockings over her long smooth legs, fixing them to the clips of her suspenders. She hesitated then, holding the black silk knickers decorated with rucked lace ready to slip over her feet and on up her legs to cover her bottom. Should she wear them? Henri had quite forcefully declared his desire that she should not wear panties. It excited him, he had said, to know she was thus secretly unclad beneath her outer garments; to know that she was bared ready to receive him. But he was not there and would not know. Jacqueline's first inclination was to obey her lover in his absence as in his presence, even though she had never quite got used to going without underwear. For a couple of minutes she struggled with this moral dilemma.

Had she then reflected on her situation - an activity which she avoided unconsciously - Jacqueline would have been astounded at how subtly, but yet how completely, Henri had invaded and taken over her life.

She had been delighted to land the job with the prestigious private banking house of Lemarchand et Freres. Even with her excellent law degree she had realised that, fresh from the Sorbonne, securing a good job would be a struggle. Her luck in getting the post promised to set her on the road to a very bright future.

It was not very long before she had had the opportunity of working closely with the virtual owner and certainly the driving force of the firm and of observing him at close quarters. Soon she came to understand why he had justly earned the reputation of being one of the most brilliant and ruthless financiers of the modern age. He dominated every situation, directed strategy with an iron grasp and wielded power without reserve. Jacqueline had adored him.

Willingly she accepted his invitation to dinner, delighted to be squired by this handsome, virile man who carried his fifty-some years so lightly. She revelled in his company, savouring his urbanity, his air of experience which translated into pleasing actuality. It was quite natural for her to go to bed with him and to find him, to her joy, a most complete, accomplished and satisfying lover. Henri Lemarchand was careful to do everything to fully pleasure Jacqueline in bed and was equally careful to ensure that she should know what would pleasure him. Jacqueline for her part was only too willing to do whatever was necessary to please this thrilling and powerful man.

Quite soon there was no place for a struggling and inexperienced young lawyer like Edouard in Jacqueline's new life. The engagement so lightly contracted was broken off as easily and poor Edouard had disappeared from the scene.

Soon Henri found it too inconvenient to visit his new mistress at the apartment she shared with two other girls. He valued their privacy and the presence of her flatmates was inhibiting. Likewise, using hotel rooms could not offer the comfort and convenience he demanded. So it was that Henri thoughtfully suggested that he should secure an apartment for Jacqueline in an appropriate district where he would feel able to visit her often and where they could relax together. In fact he knew of just the place; had indeed bought and furnished it already. So it was settled.

Later, Henri expressed the view that having his mistress working in the firm was not quite to his taste. For example, he explained persuasively, if he should wish to spend time with her and she were involved with pressing work it should not be allowed that the health of the bank should suffer and their private pleasures would have to be set aside. No, far better that he should make her an allowance privately and that she should give up her job. It all seemed perfectly reasonable and so it was settled.

Indeed, Henri did spend a good deal of time with his attractive young mistress. He would visit Jacqueline at least three times a week. He took her to dinner, to the theatre, to the races. This was no 'hole-in-the-wall' affaire and considering that she was sharing him with a wife, his family and, of course, the bank, Jacqueline enjoyed a good share of his attention. She was not unhappy with her lot.

Then he was most generous, buying her clothes, jewellery and perfume. In this, as in many other ways, Henri Lemarchand was unlike other men in that he took particular care in choosing each gift personally. Indeed, Jacqueline's lover took a great and particular interest in her appearance and adornment and was very precise in letting her know what would and would not please him. Jacqueline found this attention pleasant and flattering, not an unwelcome intrusion at all and, anyway, she was happy to do anything to please her generous and virile lover.

So she stood, still contemplating the scrap of black silk. She allowed herself a last rebellion and slipped the knickers on, shivering slightly at her own temerity. Then she finished dressing, zipping herself into a short, black jersey dress that clung to and displayed her very pleasing contours most effectively. She chose some heavy, yellow gold jewellery, earrings, a necklace and a chunky bangle - some of Henri's favourite pieces - and, slipping on her shoes, she was ready.

She was just debating with herself whether to phone ahead to book a table, when the door bell suddenly chimed.

Jacqueline opened the door to be confronted by a tall, elegant woman who was probably in her late thirties. The woman was well dressed in an understated way; designer leather trousers tucked into boots, a chunky black sweater and a slouch hat which obscured her upper face. Jacqueline remarked the woman's heavy gold jewellery which strangely mirrored her own.

"Jacqueline? Jacqueline Dupont?"

Jacqueline nodded.

"May I come in, my dear?"

Before Jacqueline could respond the woman had pushed quite brusquely past her and strode purposefully into the lounge. Jacqueline could do nothing but follow and watch as this stranger made herself comfortable in an armchair. The woman removed her hat, tossing it onto a coffee table, and shook out her long black hair to tumble loosely over her shoulders. She treated Jacqueline to a long, searching stare and, at last, spoke.

"I am glad to meet you at last Jacqueline. My name is Madeleine Lemarchand!" She paused to let the full effect register on Jacqueline before she continued in an even tone, "Come now, my girl, close your mouth. You look so undignified, gawping there like a goldfish. After all, I am only your lover's wife."

In her total astonishment Jacqueline stood rooted to the spot and stared stupidly at her quite unexpected guest. She accepted the older woman's suggestion and closed her mouth but continued to goggle in disbelief at the figure who sat calmly before her.

Madeleine crossed her legs and settled back in her seat, never once releasing Jacqueline from her steady, imperious gaze. She patted her hair back into place, perfectly in control of herself and of the situation.

"Now calm yourself my dear. Henri and I discussed you last night and we agreed that it was time that I visited you. To look you over, so to speak."

Jacqueline's vision blurred and her mind raced. She was just not understanding what this woman was saying. How could it be that Henri had left her bed to return home and 'discuss' her with his wife? The young woman's thoughts whirled. She tried to speak but nothing issued from her mouth.

Madeleine continued in the same level tones. "Since it's nearly midday I think you could offer me a little aperitif. You must have some pastis in the flat. No ice and about this much water." She indicated the required amount with thumb and forefinger. "Oh and you must have one too. It might steady you. You are positively ashen."

Quite so. The blood had drained from Jacqueline's face and she was beginning to tremble. Without thinking, as if in a dream, she went to the kitchen to prepare the drinks. Her hands shook and the glasses clinked against the bottle as she splashed a measure of the clear, yellow liquor into them. She added water, watching the pastis turn cloudy, then, clutching a glass tightly in each hand, returned on unsteady legs to confront her visitor.

Madeleine motioned her to take the seat opposite. The two women sipped their drinks and eyed each other for some minutes. Finally Jacqueline mustered her spirits enough to speak.

"I suppose you are here to tell me to leave Henri alone. Is that what this visit is for?"

The older woman smiled wryly and again in her flat calm and unemotional manner responded,

"Don't be so foolish. I have known about you and Henri from the start. There are no secrets between us. Never have been. Henri has certain needs, certain appetites. I am content that Henri should take his pleasure with a mistress such as you. As long as he tells me everything and makes sure that I too am pleased."

Realisation of the import of her comments dawned slowly and unpleasantly on Jacqueline and she flushed hotly. Could it be that Henri had informed his wife of all that had passed between them? Was it possible that everything that had taken place, as she had supposed, in the privacy of her bed, had in fact been related openly and in detail to Madeleine?

As if divining her thoughts, the older woman spoke in confirmation. "Oh yes. Henri does tell me absolutely everything. I have followed the development of your relationship with great interest. It has been fascinating to see how Henri has accustomed you to his requirements. That is why I am here. You have reached that stage of development where I can most usefully become involved."

On that enigmatic and somehow strangely threatening note Madeleine drained her glass and abruptly got to her feet.

"Now I think it is time for a little tour of inspection. Follow me!" With a proprietorial air she set off towards the kitchen. It soon became obvious that she knew the layout of the apartment intimately and had obviously been there several times before. Jacqueline, bewildered and seething with helpless annoyance at the high-handed way she was being treated, could only follow in her rival's footsteps.

The kitchen and then the bathroom were quickly inspected. Madeleine, noticing the half eaten croissant and the unwashed coffee cup, remarked that Jacqueline should take better care of herself and eat a proper breakfast. Then it was on to the bedroom where Madeleine expressed her approval that all was tidy and the bed properly made up.

The two women stood facing each other at the foot of the bed. Jacqueline was starting to feel the effect of the pastis on her empty stomach. Her head buzzed slightly and her vision was a trifle blurred. All in all this whole episode was becoming increasingly divorced from reality.

"Now let us have a good look at you," Madeleine ordered in the same matter-of-fact tone that she had used from the moment she had first appeared at Jacqueline's door. "Get undressed."

Quite naturally Jacqueline hesitated and stared hard at the other woman. Surely she had not said that?

Injecting a tone of firmness into her voice Madeleine reiterated her command. "Jacqueline, I am used to being obeyed without question or hesitation. Now do as you are told. Take off your clothes."

Jacqueline responded then. She tugged at the zipper, drew it down and stepped out of her dress. Quickly she fumbled with the catches of her bra and the creamy globes of her breasts tumbled into sight. She hooked her thumbs into the waistband of her panties and was about to draw them over her bottom and down her legs when Madeleine spoke.

"Hasn't Henri told you not to wear panties?" she asked, indicating the offending garment with a careless gesture. "They are usually one of pet hates."

"Well, yes, yes he has," stammered Jacqueline, taken completely off-guard.

"Madame! You must always address me as Madame," her oppressor corrected icily.

"Yes Madame, he did tell me not to wear them," Jacqueline responded automatically, and lowered her eyes to avoid the other woman's gaze.

"Well, at least you are honest. I was quite aware that Henri had forbidden you to wear panties. It seems, however, that your obedience needs some attention. Take them off now but leave the stockings and garter belt for the time being."

Jacqueline removed the wispy garment which now seemed to be so troublesome and stood, blushing attractively, to face her oppressor. It seemed hardly credible to her that all this was happening. Here she was confronted by a total stranger who made outrageous demands of her - and worst of all she was obeying without question. Here she was, virtually naked with that same woman's appraising eyes upon her fine porcelain pale flesh.

Madeleine had been carrying with her a large, black leather clutch bag. She rummaged in its capacious interior and brought forth a riding crop. Jacqueline's eyes opened wider yet as she saw the thin black shaft topped with a loop of pliable leather.

"I think a little taste of this will do you good. And it will prepare you for things to come in the future, as we get to know each other." Madeleine was flexing the whippy shaft.

Abject horror was written clearly on Jacqueline's face. Her lips formed a soundless 'No!'

"My dear," began Madeleine, a hint of exasperation creeping into her voice, "you really must learn that when I propose a thing then it will be so. Now I am sure that Henri has already introduced you to punishment in some forms. Am I correct?"

But of course she was correct. In his subtle and insidious fashion Henri had taken pains to introduce his attractive young mistress to the rigours of punishment over the last few months. For the most part this had consisted of a little hand spanking on her bare bottom, usually on the pretext of Jacqueline having committed some real or pretended minor misdemeanour. This was more like vigorous love play than chastisement and although her bottom glowed and stung from the firm slaps of her lover's hand this treatment also made her deliciously randy. When at last she was allowed to get up from across his knee their lovemaking was passionate and abandoned, taking them both to new heights of bliss.

On two or three other memorable occasions Jacqueline had so enraged Henri by her misconduct (which mostly took the form of not being in to receive his call or of not being ready when he came to take her to dinner or to the theatre) that he had elected to punish her more thoroughly. On these occasions she had had to strip to her stockings, kneel and beg his forgiveness and then present her bottom as he used a thick leather belt on the sensitive globes. Of course, the pain and humiliation were intense and horrible, but somehow Jacqueline could see that she deserved to be chastised thus and was quietly happy to please her lover thus if he wished to use her so. Afterwards, despite or maybe because of the fire in her glowing bottom, she gave herself with added ardour as Henri made love to her in their big cosy bed.

"Yes Madame, you are right," Jacqueline replied, still eyeing the riding crop.

With the merest hint of a smile of triumph playing over her lips, Madeleine studied her victim intently, running her eye appreciatively over the ripe curves of Jacqueline's body. Languidly she traced the curve of one opulent breast with the tip of the crop. She placed the shaft underneath the exquisite rondure to raise the flesh and let it fall back against Jacqueline's chest.

"Henri has always had a penchant for ripe, well rounded breasts. Yours are especially delicious - I am sure he pleasures himself there often."

Jacqueline coloured up even more and responded softly,

"Yes, Madame."

Madeleine reached out a long, sharp finger nail and drew it over one flaccid nipple, barely touching the sensitive bud but nevertheless sending a shiver down Jacqueline's spine. She wetted her finger tip and smeared her saliva over the pink nipple, teasing it between her fingers as, instantly, it stiffened to stand erect at the tip of the creamy globe of flesh.

Slaash! Without warning, striking like a cobra, the leather thong fell squarely across the erectile nipple, quivering the surrounding flesh. Involuntarily Jacqueline backed away and uttered a shrill cry of surprise and anguish. Instantly her hand went up to cup and comfort her poor injured bosom.

"Hands to your side," the matter-of-fact voice commanded. "Now turn slowly and let me get a good look at your bottom and those shapely thighs."

Jacqueline's face was bright scarlet, flushed with shame and embarrassment. Why was she letting this woman do this to her? Why should she obey? But obey she did, teetering on her high heels and slowly turning on the spot as her lover's wife commented admiringly on the firmness of her bottom and the shape of her thighs.

At last she had described a full circle and again came face to face with her tormentor.

"Good. Very good. And now it's time for your punishment. Kneel over that, if you please." Madeleine indicated a long, leather topped dressing stool that stood before the dressing table.

Unhesitatingly Jacqueline assumed the desired posture, kneeling at one end and stretching herself along the seat, clasping the far end.

"That's right, press your tits flat against the leather. Push your bottom up. Part your legs a little." Madeleine indicated with the crop the exact positioning required.

Very lightly then, just tickling the sensitive flesh, Madeleine drew the leathern tip of the crop over the out-thrust buttocks and the tautly thewed thighs of her victim.

"Yes, a very fine target. You have a lovely big bottom, my dear. The buttocks spread out so well. Now, reach back and part your cheeks so that I can see your bum-hole."

The enormity of this demand was just too much for Jacqueline. There was just no way on earth that she would expose herself in this way to that woman.

'Whaaak!' A searing slash of white fire burnt into her buttocks as the crop slapped down hard across the fullest flesh of her bottom. Jacqueline howled in abject misery as tears and a red mist of pain filled her eyes.

"You really must learn that I expect to be obeyed instantly. Now do as I ask," came the steady, imperious voice from behind her.

Jacqueline, with some little difficulty, groped behind herself and parted her bum-cheeks as directed, holding the flesh gingerly in a vain attempt to minimise the pain. Tickling, she felt the loop of leather caress the puckered hole of her anus and then stroke along the wide furrow of her bum cleft.

"What a lovely tight bum-hole," Madeleine commented absently. "Does Henri use you there often?" She knew very well that Henri had enjoyed his mistress in this way on many occasions, but how deliciously humiliating for her victim to have to admit it to her!

"Yes, Madame, quite often."

Jacqueline nearly choked as she gave the response. Tears welled in her eyes and she sobbed a little.

"Go on, my dear. You will shed plenty of tears before we finish," came the voice from behind her.

Expertly Madeleine again used the loop of leather to irritate the sensitive puckered hole of her victim's anus. Then, 'Flick, flick,' two quick strokes of the leather thong bit at poor Jacqueline's bum-hole, eliciting a howl of pain and causing her to contort her features in a rictus grin of discomfort.

Soft hands stroked her bum flesh, cupping the ivory hemispheres and drifting lazily over the sensitive flesh between her thighs. Those same hands released the clasp of her garter belt to allow the black stockings to roll down to her knees. Then with quick, deft flicks her tormentor began to play the leathern thong over Jacqueline's bottom, raising tiny blotches of red on the quivering, creamy flesh. With each rapid pin-prick of pain the young woman whimpered and tears began to flow. A few minutes of this treatment and her bottom stung as if she had sat on a bed of nails.

Madeleine shifted her attention to her victim's legs, flicking the thong expertly over the soft flesh of Jacqueline's inner thighs. Then, again with deft and telling flicks, Madeleine tormented the lips of her victim's unprotected sex, visiting real agony on the poor girl. By now, of course, the flinching victim was crying lustily, in floods of tears and clutching tightly, her knuckles white, to the leather topped bench.

Finally, measuring each stroke so that her victim felt each individual stripe, Madeleine thrashed the poor girl's quivering bum until the creamy flesh glowed hotly like a brazier of coals. Jacqueline was naturally in agony, feeling as if the skin was being peeled piecemeal from her poor tortured fesses.

Madeleine at last considered that her victim had suffered enough - at least for the time being - and put away the well used instrument of correction. Still without raising her voice she ordered Jacqueline to get up.

Sobbing and partially blinded by her hot, salt tears, the young woman got unsteadily to her feet. Trembling slightly, not daring to touch her stinging bottom despite her natural urge to try to comfort herself, she confronted her tormentor with as much courage as she could still muster. The loosened stockings crept over her calves to pool around her feet contriving to make her feel, if possible, even more naked and vulnerable.

Madeleine was talking to her:

"Henri was quite right. You still have some way to go before we can say you are properly trained. It is best now that you come and stay with us. I can supervise you at our house and make sure you develop along the right lines and take you in hand if necessary. It will also be more convenient for Henri when he wants you. Beside any other consideration, it is an unwarranted extravagance to keep a flat in town when we have fifteen bedrooms in the country which we barely use."

Jacqueline barely comprehended what was being said to her. Beside any other consideration, her mind was still fully occupied by the fires in her bottom and her sex.

"Get dressed now and come with me. No, you will not need to pack. We have provided clothes and other necessities for you already. Just leave this behind and come with me."

Thoroughly cowed and obedient, Jacqueline did as she was instructed and once again fully dressed she followed her mistress out of the flat and down to the waiting car in the street below.

# THE SISTERS

## I

Fifteen minutes to go! The ominous ticking of the clock in the empty, oppressively silent study-room told off the seconds until she must go to her appointment with Miss Gray. The eight hours since her interview with that individual had dragged by and now a bare fifteen minutes remained. All of her schoolmates were in class, hard at their French and Latin texts or probing the depths of modern mathematics while Julia was forced to wait alone - to wait on the time appointed.

She felt a dull ache of anticipation in the pit of her stomach. With lack-lustre gaze she watched the steady rain fall on the Scottish moorland which surrounded the school and separated it from the nearest town which lay some five miles away.

Her interview with the headmistress had been short and to the point.

"You have been here for more than three months, Julia, so you are not exactly a new girl," Miss Gray had shrilled. "Anyway, you know the rules. There is to be no consorting with the town boys. Girls of this academy are destined for better things. But you ... You abused the privilege of a Saturday afternoon visit to flaunt this cardinal rule. You were seen hand in hand, no less!"

But Alistair had been such a nice boy. Anyway nothing untoward had happened. Well Julia wouldn't allow it, would she? No, just an innocent kiss or three. Well, actually Alistair had tried to feel her blossoming breasts, but she had only let his hand rest there for a moment ...

"So, young Julia, I am afraid that I must punish you. You know what that means, don't you?"

Oh yes, Julia knew. The cane or maybe the tawse (this was Scotland after all), with Julia bent over, bottom bare, clothes up around her neck. Already she flushed hotly at the mere anticipation of the pain and humiliation. Girls of eighteen do not expect to be treated so and poor Julia had managed so far to avoid the experience. But, of course, she had heard the stories and seen the results.

"I will not inflict the punishment now. No, I find that time to reflect is beneficial and will make you appreciate your chastisement even more. You will come here at four o'clock, properly prepared."

Eight hours. Eight long, gloom filled hours, all filled with bitter anticipation of the pain and embarrassment to come.

"You share a study room with Aimee, Amanda and Natasha, do you not?"

"Yes Miss," Julia had stammered.

Indeed, since she had come as a boarder to this school some three months before she had been befriended, almost adopted, by the three girls that Miss Gray had mentioned. The life of a boarding school had been strange and unfamiliar to Julia then, having been a day girl for all of her school career. Then her father had had to go to the States just at the critical point in her preparation for university entrance - a place at Oxford was certainly expected for her. Boarding school seemed to offer the best solution and Julia knew how lucky she had been to get her place at St. Monica's.

"Ah yes, 'The Sisters'," Miss Gray murmured musingly. "Good. They all know what is required. They will instruct you how to prepare and how to conduct yourself. Now off you go."

"Oh my poor darling," sighed sweet little Natasha when Julia told her friends of her sentence. "To be beaten and for so little. Your poor dear bottom to be covered in wicked bruises."

"Never mind. Then you really will be one of us," cut in Aimee.

"What do you mean?" asked Julia, all innocence.

"One of 'The Sisters' silly. It's sort of a rite of initiation. We've all had beatings from Miss Gray. You'll see, just wait," she added with a slight air of mystery in her voice. Julia nodded thoughtfully while not understanding the import of her friend's words at all.

"Anyway," Aimee went on, "that will be just perfect because anyone can see that poor Natasha has a terrific crush on you."

"Oh yes, dear girl," sighed Natasha breathily, "I'd take the beating for you if I could."

"But you can't, so stop behaving like a lovesick child," chimed in Amanda as she sat on one of the study desks and idly swung her stockinged legs back and forth. "Let's be practical. I suppose Miss Gray said that we would show you how to prepare and how to behave?"

Julia, still trembling inside at the very thought of what the whippy rattan cane or leather tawse would do to her bottom in a few short hours, gloomily agreed.

"Good," Amanda carried on, "that's a good sign. You just do as we tell you and everything will be fine. You'll still have to be caned and you'll have a sore bum. Miss Gray isn't noted for her leniency. But then you will see that things will be just fine."

It seemed that the first rule was that Miss Gray liked her victims to be well groomed and smartly turned out, at least to the standard expected for chapel or on Parent's Day.

At lunchtime, at Aimee's insistence, Julia showered again, washing her long hair and making sure that fingernails and so on were all scrupulously clean. Then Natasha brushed Julia's rich auburn hair until it shone; one hundred strokes of the mother-of-pearl handled brush each side, mewling with pity at her 'poor darling's' fate all the while.

Then it was time to dress in her best, Sunday and Founder's Day only, strictly regulation school uniform. Julia was glad as she slipped the soft, white cotton pants up her slim legs and over her ripe bottom, that they weren't of the terrible, old-fashioned blue serge bloomer type one might have expected. At least she would not be too embarrassed by the style of her undergarments when she had to lift her skirts.

In fact St. Monica's uniform was not too bad at all. Yes, it was functional and greys and whites dominated, but the cut was quite chic and quite figure flattering.

Julia buttoned up her crisp, freshly pressed white blouse then slipped the regulation grey cotton gym-slip over her head. The pleated skirt hung well, hugging her juvenile curves, stopping just above the knee. The final touch was a broad belt which emphasised the incurve of her waist and set off the blooming of her youthful figure which now hovered on the delightful cusp of girlishness and of mature womanhood.

Although allowed for day wear, stockings were not permitted for 'punishment parade'. But, as Julia thought, the regulation white ankle socks, turned down a regulation two inches of cuff, were not too horrible. Especially when set off by the smart, low heeled, patent leather shoes.

"Now for how you must behave when you are in there with the Head," Amanda began, when Julia was fully dressed. "Listen very carefully because it's all essential."

"First, be punctual to the second. Then do exactly as Miss Gray tells you. Don't hesitate, don't argue, just do it. And don't do anything without her instruction. You just stand or bend over or whatever else she tells you to do. Remember, she's in charge.

"When she's caning you, don't be afraid to yell out. It'll help you to cope with the pain and show her that she's doing you some good. Feedback she calls it.

"But whatever you do, don't blub. Crying is only for little kids - in front of Miss Gray anyway. Hang on to your tears, bite your lip and then you can have a good blub here with us. Natasha will enjoy that!" and Amanda grinned wryly.

"Last point. When it's over, make sure you thank her. Nothing effusive, just, 'Thank you Miss Gray. I have learned my lesson.' OK? ... Oh yes, I nearly forgot - speak only when Miss Gray prompts you but then speak up clearly, OK?"

Julia nodded her understanding. It was bad enough being under sentence, bad enough having to wait long hours under the shadow but to have to listen to details of how she must behave as the wicked cane slashed over her bottom! Well, that was just too horrible. Her eyes misted and her underlip began to quiver.

Very gently, Aimee took her hand and gave a friendly, comforting squeeze. "Don't take on so. Try to relax. Be brave and you'll be fine. Then, I promise you, we'll have some great times."

Then there was nothing to do but wait. The first hour was fine. 'The Sisters' stayed with her since all of them had a free period for private study. Some gentle horseplay and conversation in lowered tones helped to pass the time. Then her friends had to go off to last period, which was French. Julia, being under sentence, was excused.

So, prepared like a bride to meet her fate, poor Julia sat looking bleakly out of the window as rain lashed the Scottish countryside. She tried to read but her mind would not focus. All there was was a dark tunnel and at the end Miss Gray, pain and humiliation.

The hands of the clock dragged themselves sluggishly through those last fifteen minutes. With two minutes to go Julia got herself to her feet and set off.

Her footsteps echoed along the empty, dusty corridors, filling the ominous silence of the school. At four o'clock precisely she stood before Miss Gray's door and tapped gently. She obeyed the muffled summons to enter and stood confronting her tormentor.

For what seemed to be an age Miss Gray subjected the unfortunate, almost trembling girl to a searching scrutiny of her appearance. At last, seemingly satisfied with what she saw, the headmistress broke the silence.

"Very good, young lady. At least you are punctual and you seem to have prepared yourself properly. Now, take off your tunic and your pants. You can fold them - neatly mind - on that chair. Then roll up your blouse so that I can have a clear field of operations."

"Nooo! Oh no!" poor Julia's confused brain revolted. She would be virtually naked, everything on display! She had not expected this - just taking down her pants would have been bad enough.

"Come along girl, don't dawdle."

Julia's fingers fumbled at her belt, tripped over the buttons of her gym-slip. Quickly she drew down the soft, chastely white underpants and rolled the blouse neatly to just below her bra. Again she stood to suffer the cold scrutiny of the headmistress.

She felt Miss Gray's gaze upon her, taking in the dip of her waist, following the delicate swell of her belly beneath the oversize dimple of her navel, down to the sweet auburn tuft at the confluence of her slim thighs. She had never felt more naked, more shamefully exposed. Poor Julia flushed hotly and gazed at the carpet with savage intensity.

"Now Julia," Miss Gray began again, "I have decided to cane you." Here she picked up and flourished a wicked looking rattan cane, still whippy despite its apparent thickness.

"Place your feet here," indicating a spot on the floor with the tip of the cane. "Bend over the desk and grasp the far edge. That's right - now you are properly braced."

Obediently Julia stretched over the desk and pressed her bosom and bare belly into its cold wooden surface. Tapping her ankles with the cane, Miss Gray indicated that her victim should spread her legs slightly. Thus, her legs parted in a perfect inverted V, Julia hugged the desk, blushingly aware that all of her intimate parts were now fully on display. The tension in her thighs began to tell and Julia's legs began to tremble. Desperately she fought to master herself.

Long moments passed as the head mistress again quite pointedly admired the sight of the helpless girl, even passing her hand over Julia's ripe buttocks to test the tension of the muscle. At last, satisfied that her victim was prepared, Miss Gray placed the tip of the rod on the very apex of Julia's perfectly ovate bottom, measuring the distance.

"I have decided that you shall suffer eighteen strokes of the cane. Brace yourself!"

Julia groaned within herself. Eighteen strokes! Oh no! She felt the tip of the cane leave her bottom - a pause - then the rattan cleaved the air with a swish and thwacked crisply athwart Julia's fleshy moons. A blur of agony flashed through her loins to fill her senses to the exclusion of all other thought or sensation. Julia's whole world was hot and red and filled with hurt. As the clouds of pain rolled away, she heard Miss Gray:

"I expect you are hoping that we can rattle through the remaining seventeen strokes quickly now. I am afraid that will not be the case. I must make each stroke count to be sure you obtain the full benefit. Do you understand?"

"Yes Miss Gray." But her bum was on fire already.

The pain of the first stroke had just about abated to a dull throb when the cane again swished through the silent, heavy air and cracked harshly on bare buttock flesh. Julia jerked and yelled involuntarily.

"That's right my dear. Let me hear how much good I am doing you."

Slowly, inexorably, methodically, the punishment progressed. The cane slashed viciously again and again over Julia's quivering fesses which soon turned to one ruddy mass of soreness. Such, however, was Miss Gray's skill that each stroke was clearly discernible to her victim and called forth a satisfying response from Julia's healthy, young lungs.

"There, my dear," the voice of her tormentor broke through the crimson veil of pain. "You've enjoyed nine already. Half way through. Are you feeling properly chastised?"

Tears were beginning to well up, choking at her throat, flooding her eyes, but bravely Julia fought them down, biting her lip until she had control. Grasping tightly on the desk, with a slight tremor in her voice, she answered:"Yes, Miss Gray. My bottom is really agony. I am very, very sorry for what I did."

"That's as it should be. Bravely now and we'll get on."

Again the whippy rattan whistled through the air and connected with Julia's sorely tormented bottom. A pause, the immediate pain subsiding to the dull throb which formed the background of the poor victim's sensations. Then again wood and flesh made harsh contact, the cane striping across the tender flesh where upper thigh curves to meet the luscious globe of the buttock.

Julia yelled with the pain and jigged from one foot to the other, still fighting the tears.

Thus, in the same vein, the punishment continued until the full tally of strokes had been visited across Julia's pain filled backside. Julia, her lower lip almost bitten through, fighting to control the muscle spasm in her thighs and calves, had inevitably failed to keep count of the tally of strokes as her ordeal had progressed but simply lay prostrate across the headmistress' desk until told to stand.

She remembered the instructions: 'Don't forget to thank her.'

Fighting back the urge to clasp her bottom in order somehow relieve the hurt, Julia stood, her head bowed, to face her tormentor.

"Thank you Miss Gray for punishing me. I be-be-believe that I have learned my lesson," she managed to blurt out.

"Very good, Julia. Get dressed now and get along to your study. I am sure 'The Sisters' will be anxious to see you."

Julia needed no urging. Gathering her wits about her she was dressed in seconds flat and with a hasty nod of the head to Miss Gray in acknowledgement of her dismissal she was through the door to the safety of the corridor in no time at all.

On legs which had suddenly become made of rubber, her bottom clenched against the bitter throb that invested her poor tormented nates, Julia tottered back along the still silent corridor. Almost blinded by the salty tears which welled up in her eyes she all but fell through the study door into the comforting arms of dear Aimee.

Safe at last, with welcome release she buried her head in the other girl's bosom and gave herself up to weeping.

For long minutes the two girls stood in the middle of the room while Aimee's gentle embrace enfolded Julia to draw her into her soft warmth, her hands gently massaging her back as deep sobs wracked the suffering girl. At last Julia came to herself and raised her head from her friend's tear wet blouse to smile gratefully into the face of her comforter.

"There, my dear, not so bad after all. I'm sure a good cry has helped. It did for me the first time. We've got some lovely soothing cream that will ease your pains. You'll be fine, just fine."

The soft words murmuring in her ears, Julia became aware for the first time that Amanda and Natasha were also present.

"Slip off your things and we'll have a look at the damage."

No embarrassment here. It seemed the most natural thing in the world for Julia to doff her gym-slip and draw her pants over the tender globes of her buttocks and down her legs to display her bruised bottom to her sympathetic friends. After all, they had all seen each other in the buff often enough, in the shower, in the dorm.

"Kneel up here on the armchair so we can see in the light."

Just as she had done for Miss Gray but now without thinking, Julia rolled up her blouse to properly bare her lower body and arranged herself facing the back of the chair. Amanda fetched a mirror and held it so that Julia too could join in the inspection of her wounded bum. As would be expected, her entire rump was a mass of glowing red as the eighteen individual stripes had coalesced into one hurtful mass. Here and there, though, also stood a deep blue-black bruise where the cane had struck the flesh especially hard.

"Hmmm, quite a pasting. I hope you remembered to behave just as we told you."

Julia, with a quiet pride, assured them that she had.

"Right," went on Amanda, "let's have the cream. Natasha, I'm sure would love to do the honours."

Of course she would! The slim, blonde girl hurried to fetch the jar of soothing cream that stood on the study room table.

The first contact of the cream on Julia's burning flesh was delicious, the thick dab of ointment forming a pool of soothing coolness as it lay on her buttock. Then gently, very gently, her hands fluttering over her darling's inflamed flesh, Natasha spread the healing balm to cover poor Julia's throbbing bum-flesh. This treatment contrasted delectably with the earlier experiences and Julia gave herself up to luxurious enjoyment of her friend's touch.

Then she became aware, all at once, that Natasha's soft hands had left her bottom and had been replaced by her lips and tongue. Ecstatically the girl lavished kisses on her darling's ruddy fesses and drew her moist little tongue over the smooth, silken skin. Little by little Natasha trailed her tiny pink asp over Julia's globes, approaching nearer and nearer to the cleft between the cheeks then licking voluptuously up and down the secret crevice, probing with the point of her tongue, parting the cheeks.

The sensations between Julia's legs were hotly, sensually liquid. Unthinkingly she began to give herself up to this new sensation. Luxuriating in the gentle grasp of Natasha's hand on her hip, the soft, wet caress of lips and tongue over her abused flesh. Unconsciously one hand slipped towards her brimming sex, began to probe ...

"That's quite enough 'Tasha. You're both getting carried away and you don't have permission yet!" Amanda broke in on the magical moment.

Obediently Natasha left off her ministrations and Julia came to earth with a bump. Natasha went back to delicately massaging her friend's bottom, kneading the soothing ointment deep into her aching fesses until, at length, Julia was overcome by a pleasant drowsiness and lapsed into a light sleep, curled in the armchair, a comforting thumb between her lips.

II

"You see? We told you everything would be fine," Amanda exclaimed as she knelt in front of the gas fire making the breakfast toast.

It was one of the privileges of being a member of the Upper Sixth at St. Monica's that girls were allowed to take their breakfast in the shared study rooms rather than in the communal hurly-burly of the school refectory. 'The Sisters' quite naturally availed themselves of any privilege that would set them apart from the common herd. Every day, therefore, began with tea and toast, taken together in the dusty study room that the four girls shared.

This morning the start of day ritual had been slightly disturbed by the arrival of a breathless first year girl carrying a note from Miss Gray.

'Trouble in store!' was Julia's immediate first thought as she remembered her humiliating encounter with the headmistress and the very sore bottom that had been the outcome of that interview. Aimee on the contrary, with every indication of excited pleasure, tore open the small brown envelope and read out loud:

"'The Sisters' are invited to take tea with The Headmistress at 6.30 pm today at School House. Julia is, of course, to be included in the party."

The note was signed 'P Gray, Headmistress.'

Several days had passed since Julia had been caned by Miss Gray. The soreness in her poor punished bottom had totally subsided and an early morning inspection of her bottom using a small hand-mirror had revealed no trace of a bruise on the soft, ivory flesh. In that time Julia had tried to put the incident from her mind - both the beating and what had so nearly followed afterwards with sweet, pretty Natasha. It was difficult, however, and she found herself, almost unconsciously, reliving those painful but strangely exciting events, especially when she was alone at night curled in her warm bed. Yes, there was an element of excitement attached to what had happened. As she relived the harsh contact of the cane on her bumflesh, the humiliation of her near nudity under the scrutiny of Miss Gray, the intimate caress of Natasha's lips and tongue, she felt herself grow moist between her slender thighs. Her hand, almost of itself, would creep down to relieve the tension ...

The time appointed for their attendance on the headmistress soon came around and 6.30 found the four girls, all smartly turned out in their 'Sunday Chapel' uniforms, walking through the chilly gloom of a November evening towards 'School House'.

The small, grey stone cottage which was the residence of St. Monica's headmistress stood a little removed from the rest of the school buildings over by the school gates. Its position ensured that the headmistress was always within easy reach of the school and her charges but preserved her privacy during her times of relaxation.

Inside, the warm and welcoming living room was not at first view furnished in a style that would be thought of as typical of the quarters of the headmistress of a well-reputed school for girls. A large and capacious couch, easily capable of accommodating two people lying side by side, dominated the room. No other seating was provided, instead a number of large, well stuffed cushions or beanbags were strewn at random about the floor for guests to recline or sit upon as they wished. The walls were hung with a curious collection of tapestries, paintings and artefacts of West African origin. The lighting was subdued, in fact most of the light was provided by the cheerful open fire that warmed the room so invitingly after the chill of the November night.

Once admitted to the house, the three girls, Amanda, Natasha and Aimee displayed an easy familiarity with these surroundings, flopping down on the cushions and chatting with Miss Gray in an easy and unaffected manner. Julia was not at all surprised. After all, Aimee had explained that these gatherings were quite a regular event and were much enjoyed and looked forward to. For her own part, however, being unsure of how best to behave, Julia sat primly, back straight and posture formal, on the edge of the couch.

Miss Gray too, now that Julia had time to look about her, no longer had the appearance normally associated with the headmistress of a school of such academic excellence and cachet as St. Monica's. Her ash blonde hair which she normally wore gathered tightly at the back of her head was now let down in a lustrous chignon that glinted palely in the low light. Her face, normally innocent of cosmetics, was carefully made up - her high cheek bones emphasised by blusher, her striking green eyes highlighted by carefully understated eyeshadow. A subtle aroma of French perfume surrounded her. Her clothes too were no longer the plain adornment of the serious educator. Instead she wore an elegant blouse of fine grey silk, open at the neck and thrust into the top of loosely cut black lounging pants. Her bare feet were curled beneath her as she lounged on a pile of cushions. In short, like a butterfly, a maturely beautiful woman had emerged from the chrysalis of the serious and severe headmistress.

Smiling and making small talk, Miss Gray dispensed tea and cake from the collation that was set out on a low table which, the sofa apart, was the only piece of furniture in the room. She was in every way a charming and considerate hostess, so much in contrast with the serious mentor who had so punished poor Julia but a few short days ago.

Julia began to relax, enveloped by the cosy warmth and embraced by the light-hearted chaffing of her schoolfellows and by Miss Gray's more serious probing about progress towards the University entrance exams that would take place at the end of the Summer term. She sipped her Earl Grey tea and nibbled at the generous slice of Dundee cake with which she had been served. Suddenly she realised that the headmistress was addressing her,

"Tell me Julia, my dear, have you recovered from the little punishment I was forced to give you the other day?"

Surprised by the sudden reference to an event she had thought forgotten, Julia could barely stammer her response, "Yes thank you, Miss Gray."

"No, no, my dear. Here we are not on formal terms. You must call me Pamela. I like to think that here I am more like an elder sister to you," smiled the headmistress benignly.

Nonplussed, Julia could only nod her acquiescence. It did not matter. Miss Gray, or rather Pamela, continued. "That little event had an importance for you far beyond simply punishing your silly misdemeanour. It was also a final test of your metal, of your worthiness to be one of my special girls.

"Now I am sure you are only too aware that Aimee, Amanda and Natasha are certainly the most attractive girls - perhaps I should say young ladies - in the Upper School. You, my dear Julia, share that distinction.

"It must also be said that academically you four also share the laurels. So, you have both brains and beauty; our last test showed that you had metal in your character. So like the other 'Sisters' I want to have you as one of my special girls

"You should understand that that is why I was most particular in enforcing our rule about not fraternising with the common boys of the town. My special girls are destined for finer things and for more rewarding experiences. As you shall see."

Julia quite naturally was dumbstruck. This was a very strange speech in any circumstance but coming from Miss Gray, the headmistress ...

"I see that you are still a little confused," Pamela continued softly, still with the benign smile playing about her full, crimson rouged lips. "You four girls are on the verge of becoming beautiful young women. You are all very intelligent and very well educated in the academic sense. Without doubt you will all secure places at our more exalted Universities and have bright careers before you.

"I believe, however, that the academic system is not thorough enough in providing for you. In effect I believe that my special girls deserve something more. So I hold these little get-togethers so we can have some informal er ... instruction."

As she spoke Amanda and Aimee left the nest of cushions on which they had been perched and drew close to Pamela's side. Tenderly Miss Gray took Aimee's hand in both of hers as Amanda, not to be outdone, slipped her arm about the headmistress' slim waist.

"You see, my dear, my objective is to make sure that you value yourself and in future life derive the fullest pleasure from the self-knowledge I hope to inculcate in you. I want to try to put you in touch with your own sexuality; to show you the delight you are able to give to others and, in turn, to receive from them. In fine, to show you how to enjoy yourself and others to the fullest without shame and without accepting the second best or tawdry.

"It would be so easy for you to gain experiences with some common fellow that would leave you disappointed and ashamed. So easy for man in general - society if you wish - to impose their standards on you to the detriment of your own self. Here, on the other hand, you can experiment and pleasure yourself surrounded by your loving 'Sisters'. Here you may share delight openly and without either jealousy or shame."

It would be an understatement to say that Julia was stunned. Miss Gray's - Pamela's - words were certainly not those of a headmistress and the increasingly intimate caresses that Pamela now received from Amanda and Aimee were not typical of relations between teacher and pupil. What on earth was happening to her?

"My dear, I can see from your expression that a practical demonstration will probably help you to understand. You are aware, I am sure, that Natasha has a 'crush' on you?"

In the silence that followed Julia felt constrained to answer. By some miracle her tongue unglued itself.

"Yes, yes...Pamela. It is fairly obvious."

"In which case do you think you might reciprocate her desire for you?"

At this point Natasha who had stayed where she had settled herself when the other two 'Sisters' had cosied up to Miss Gray treated Julia to a winsome smile. Blue eyes, bobbed blonde hair and a beseeching look would win the day. Julia automatically answered,

"Oh yes. Certainly."

"There Natasha, Julia is willing. And now you have my permission."

Without further encouragement Natasha was on her feet. Approaching Julia she took her hand and drew her to her feet. Smiling, her wide blue eyes gazing rapturously into her beloved's, she stroked Julia's hair then, cupping her face gently, kissed her softly on the mouth. Gradually the kiss became bolder, Natasha's lips nibbled at Julia's, the probing tip of the blonde nymph's tongue stroked over Julia's mouth seeking entry. Julia succumbed, opening to the probing, insistent asp; tongues sucked and they were kissing passionately, deeply.

Breaking from the kiss, Natasha busied herself with Julia's clothing, assertive fingers unbuttoning the crisp white blouse and tugging it free from the waistband of her skirt. Insistently Natasha took Julia's hand and drew it to the top button of her own blouse.

"Help me to undress too, my darling," she whispered.

Julia's mind whirled, her eyes were unfocussed and her thoughts raced. How could she be doing this? In front of the other girls, in front of Miss Gray! But she wanted to; wanted to enjoy sweet Natasha and to have Natasha enjoy her. What could be so wrong? The kiss, tongues sucking, lips gentling lips, had been so nice. This was so ... so exciting. Why not?

Julia's fingers unfroze. Quickly, nimbly, she unfastened the blouse and drew it from Natasha's shoulders. Reaching behind she unclipped her lover's bra, drew it down her arms to bare her small, round, supple breasts. Natasha in her turn stripped her friend's upper garments from her so they were both naked to the waist. Another embrace, tongues locking, lips sucking, warmly soft breast flesh crushed together nipple on nipple.

Natasha, locked in that embrace, was still busy as she released Julia's skirt which slipped from her, pooling around her feet. The petite blonde girl slipped to her knees and hooked her thumbs in the waistband of the white cotton panties, drawing this last garment over Julia's bottom and down her slender legs. Julia stepped from her clothes and was naked. Tentatively Natasha's wetly pink tongue probed the auburn curls on Julia's Mons. Then more boldly she licked at the pudenda, moistening the pubic bush and sending tiny spasms through Julia's body.

Over the head of the kneeling girl Julia could now see her companions and Miss Gray as they reclined on a nest of cushions across the room from her. Both girls were already naked. Slender athletic Aimee - captain of lacrosse, captain of athletics - lower limbs twined about Miss Gray; well fleshed Amanda, endowed already with the full breasts of a mature woman, her arms flung about the older woman's neck. Pamela's blouse now gaped open revealing perfect, bra-less breasts, their ivory firmness needing no support as they jutted proudly amidst the crumpled grey silk. Already the coral nipples stood erect and swollen in evidence of the attentions of the two girls' lips and fingers.

163

Natasha got to her feet and slipped off the rest of her clothes to stand pinkly naked. Taking Julia's hand again she gently drew her down beside her onto another pile of cushions. Limbs entwined, breasts and bellies meeting, caressing. Hands ran riot, exploring, teasing, gentling, buttocks were cupped and pinched, breasts fondled, warmly soft inner thighs caressed.

Natasha's hand found her lover's pubic mound and gently squeezed the auburn furred plumpness. Her fingers probed further yet and found the lust swollen lips of Julia's sex and parting them plunged into the fluid depths. Julia groaned as spasms of joy climbed from her sex to her reeling brain. Natasha gently, surely, began to frig two fingers in and out as her friend luxuriated in the novel sensations obsessing her body.

Natasha's mouth was busy. Plucking at the tiny girlish nipples at the tip of Julia's nascent breasts she excited the red nubs to tumescence. Lower and lower the blonde nymph worked her tongue, laving her companion's midriff and dipping into the cup of her navel. Then lower still, trailing moistness over Julia's belly and over her pubic mound.

Then she was withdrawing her fingers, coated with her friend's love-spending, and substituting mouth and tongue. The pink, wet probe slipped between Julia's sex lips, slurping at her juices as they flooded from her. Mouth on sex, Natasha eagerly sucked at her lover's quim. Parting the labiae with sensitive fingers, Natasha brought to light the hooded nub of Julia's clitoris. Delicately at first but then with increasing urgency she lashed the tiny, sensitive nodule with her tongue. Julia gave herself up completely to the electric, sexual thrills that throbbed through her. Lying on her back, soft animal groans, little cries of "Oh, oh, oooh!" bubbled in her throat.

The two girls were now ignored by the others, who lay in a tangle of groping, writhing limbs, across the room. Pamela's head was clasped between soft, white thighs as she tongued urgently at Amanda's passion swollen womanhood. Aimee's face was thrust between the headmistress' buttocks, her tongue moistening the sensitive, puckered anal ring while Amanda's fingers squirmed wetly in her sex. The air was filled with pleasured shrieks and grunts.

Natasha increased the intensity of her tongue lashing at Julia's sexual centre. Wave after wave of climax flooded through the auburn haired beauty as she writhed on the cushions until a final cathartic pulse shuddered through her and she screamed, "Yess! Oh yesss!"

The sweet tension of her climax ebbing from her, her head spinning from the intensity of the unfamiliar sensations, Julia relaxed into the pile of cushions. Then through the mists of satiety came the urgent entreaty, whispered in her ear,

"Love me now. Please, please. Now." And she felt her hand grasped and placed between warm thighs, against labiae damp already with the dew of love.

Rousing herself, Julia exchanged places with her companion. Natasha, with a deep sigh of pleasurable relief lay prone and parted her legs for Julia to lower her head between her thighs. Untutored, following her instinct, inflamed by the musky perfume of her friend's liquid womanhood, Julia began her ministrations. Slowly she licked over the suave flesh of Natasha's inner thigh, drawing a trail of wetness closer and closer to the shrine of Venus. Then, for the first time, her tongue probed the nether lips of another's sex, plunging into the blonde girl's quim as she whimpered with pleasure and raised her hips encouraging the intimacy.

Soon Julia's busy lips found and closed over the writhing girl's clitoris, sucked on that love button, thrilling her to the depths of her loins. Soon the debt of pleasure was repaid in fullest measure as a thundering climax roared within Natasha. The girls sprawled together in a tangle of limbs as the sexual tension ebbed deliciously from them.

A soft hand caressed her tummy and gentled her breast, intruding on Julia's sated reverie. A hint of perfume curled in her nostrils. Julia opened her eyes. There, crouched above her, tips of full ivory globes just brushing the flaccid teats of Julia's breasts, her face flushed, was Pamela. The headmistress bent lower and gently kissed her mouth which was still smeared with Natasha's spicy emissions.

"My, but you are a lovely girl. Such smooth skin, such firm, budding breasts. Oh and that lovely auburn hair. You and Natasha seem to have enjoyed each other immensely."

Murmured assent and nods of agreement came from both girls. For a while all of them lounged in a companionable silence, basking in the afterglow of their carnal satisfaction. Someone put on some music and the gentle strains of a Mozart sonata filled the room. Murmured conversations began, caresses were exchanged. Miss Gray raised herself on her elbow and spoke:

"I think we should show our new sister, Julia, some of the other ways in which we pleasure ourselves. Amanda, be a dear and fetch our 'toys'."

Generously fleshed buttocks jiggling, Amanda hurried out of the room into the adjoining bedroom, bent on her errand. She returned shortly, carrying in one hand a leather paddle, fairly thick and about the shape of a ping-pong bat. In the other hand she grasped a perfect replica of an erect male organ sculpted in flesh coloured rubber.

"I am sure, dear Julia," Miss Gray continued, "that your recent visit to my office left you feeling both hurt and humiliated. That was after all the intention."

Julia's buttocks clenched and she winced at the memory.

"Cuddle up with Natasha now and let us show you that, by contrast, a certain amount of punishment - lovingly applied - can bring joy and pleasure to both the giver and the receiver."

With these words Miss Gray got to her feet and placing a couple of cushions in the middle of the sofa arranged herself on them so that her smooth, creamy white buttocks were raised up to receive. Without a word, as if playing out a well practised ritual, Amanda and Aimee took up their positions. Slender Aimee placed herself at Pamela's head, leaning back against the arm of the sofa and spreading her legs to present her pussy to her lover's mouth. Amanda, putting the dildo to one side, took up her position armed with the paddle.

"Now let me have it and none of your love pats mind. Make me feel it."

With these words Miss Gray buried her face in Aimee's sex with her nose pressed hard to the richly furred Mons.

Amanda took her admonition to heart and crashed the leather paddle hard over Pamela's upturned nates. Involuntarily, as the blow fell, Pamela jerked her hips but nevertheless continued to slurp hungrily at Aimee's pussy as if the blow had been a soft caress.

'Whaak!' Amanda increased the force she used. Pamela's ripe buttock flesh shuddered and blushed hotly while a low moan - of approval?- growled in her throat.

Another couple of whacks placed heartily one on either cheek again evinced the same reaction. Amanda paused to run her hands over the hot, red bumflesh, letting her fingers probe at the crevice between the cheeks.

"Hmm, they're getting nice and warm."

Julia was amazed. How could Miss Gray be enjoying this? With her amazement, however, also came a growing excitement. The human tableau was so overwhelmingly lustful! Delicate fingers probed at her own sex and Natasha's digits buried themselves up to the knuckle in Julia's drooling orifice. Mmm, divine!

Amanda was plying the paddle again. Miss Gray's gorgeous bottom trembled under the impact and now real, full throated cries of pain and of pleasure were drawn from her. Aimee's pussy was temporarily forgotten as the punishment progressed.

Once again the plumply beautiful Amanda stopped to fondle the crimson flesh of her victim's bottom. A finger crept between the buttocks. It tickled Pamela's anus then insinuated itself fully into the tight passage.

Pamela let out a growl of unbridled lust. Oh yes, she was certainly enjoying this!

Withdrawing her finger, Amanda continued. Leather beat upon flesh, Natasha's fingers wriggled inside Julia, Julia returned the compliment and Miss Gray squealed her pleasure.

Her face flushed as red as her victim's throbbing fesses and perspiring a little with her efforts, Amanda put down the paddle. She licked a stray droplet of sweat from her upper lip.

"There, you're nearly done. Nice and crimson all over," she commented as, once again, she ran an admiring hand over the prone woman's smooth buttocks.

"Mmm! That was lovely! Just right. Now I want you to stuff me, you sweet little bitch. Up my arse-hole first," Miss Gray purred, her voice thick with lust.

Amanda grabbed up the flesh coloured dildo and started to strap it to her groin. Julia, through half-lidded, passion dimmed eyes now got a proper look at the rubber phallus. It was in fact double ended. At one end a perfect replica of a well sized but not massive male organ, dome, glans and veins all finely crafted. The other end, set at right angles and equally thick was designed to fit into the wearer's own vagina.

With evident pleasure Amanda fitted the rubber probe into her cunt and fixed the straps about her waist to turn herself into an ersatz hermaphrodite with a well filled cunt and jutting erect male organ. Indeed the dildo jutted strangely from below the soft swell of her womanly belly as it nestled at her pubic bush. She anointed the head with spittle from her mouth and climbed up onto the sofa between Pamela's legs. Parting the bum cleft with one hand and presenting the head of the dildo with the other, she fixed the tip in the tightly elastic anal ring. Gently, grasping Pamela's hips, she pushed against the engine at her groin to slowly and inexorably drive it into her victim's bumhole until the whole length was tightly fixed within the headmistress' fundament.

Miss Gray winced and let out a soft squeal as the shaft breached the tight ring of her anus. Then as pleasure supplanted pain and Amanda began to work the dildo inside her she smiled beatifically and went back to tonguing Aimee's sweet, girlish pussy.

The lewdity of all that was taking place before her enthralled gaze had already made Julia's head spin and her pulses pound. Her emotions were in a whirl. Natasha intensified the frigging of her fingers in Julia's sex in sympathy with the bawdy frolics that were being enacted on the sofa. Julia followed suit and rapidly their mutual masturbation urged both girls to the edge of a shattering climax.

Spasms of pleasure centred on her cunt flowed through Julia's body and intensified until a shuddering, thundering climax broke over her. Natasha was not far behind and, exhausted, the two girls slumped back on their bed of cushions to watch languidly as their companions, in a frenzy of lust, worked themselves towards their own release.

Amanda still pounded lustily in Miss Gray's fundament. As she thrust in and out of the tight, clasping hole the bung in her own cunt pleasured her. The intensity of her fucking was mirrored in her own sex and spurred her on to ever greater efforts. A sheen of sweat covered her skin which glistened in the low light.

"My cunt, girl! In my cunt now!" grunted Miss Gray.

Obediently the girl withdrew from her partner's bumhole and thrust easily into the other, more conventional orifice, barely losing a beat in her fucking frenzy.

Suddenly Aimee was coming, grinding her cunt and her mossy pubis into Pamela's face. Screaming her release she clasped her compact titties and kneaded the bare handfuls of flesh as spasm after spasm rocked her frame.

Pamela too was overcome by a heady climax, growling her pleasure as her body shuddered in the grip of her release. Finally as she relaxed, Amanda found her own catharsis and the entire tableau relaxed into a torpid tangle of flesh.

The insistent chiming of the clock on the mantelpiece as it struck nine o'clock roused them from their sated reverie. Pamela, raising herself on one elbow, surveyed her charges through the curtain of her dishevelled mane of blonde hair.

"It's getting late. You'll need your beauty sleep tonight and you must be fresh for class tomorrow. Get your clothes on, my darlings, and off you go."

Languidly, unwillingly, the four girls pulled themselves together and dressed themselves. Miss Gray draped a silk robe about her delicious and well pleasured form. In a few minutes they were ready and with a flurry of quick and tender kisses and whispered thanks, the girls plunged into the cold night.

# III

The Autumn term wore on and Christmas drew near. Julia as the weeks passed took part in several more of Miss Gray's little educational get-togethers along with her 'Sisters'. On each occasion her experience was broadened and her enjoyment of her own body and of those of her friends deepened. It was not long before she was made to experience the paddle on her own quivering bum-flesh and she quickly learned just how it was indeed possible to enjoy such an exhilarating experience.

Over those weeks too, a deep bond of affection and trust developed between Julia and the attractive, sophisticated woman she had first encountered as a stern and business-like disciplinarian. Fortunately, through Pamela Gray's careful management of the group's relationships no jealousy or other negative emotion among the 'Sisters' attended on this attachment. So the girls shared in a communal affection which was unsullied by either shame or rivalry.

In this delightful atmosphere the term drew to a close and Aimee, Natasha and Amanda each departed to spend the Christmas holiday with their families. Julia was destined to join her father in New York, but was unable to get on a flight until some days after the end of term.

Of course, it was natural that Miss Gray, acting in loco parentis, should extend the hospitality of School House to her pupil. It was agreed then, that Julia should spend the few days before her departure as Pamela's house guest.

Those few days passed all too quickly in a cloud of affection and contentment. Miss Gray took on the role of elder sister with relish. During the daytime and evenings they enjoyed a variety of pleasures. They went off to Edinburgh to shop, attended concerts and the ballet and dined together. At every turn Pamela was ready with helpful advice or a comment which enriched the experience for Julia and broadened her education. At night they shared the headmistress' soft, warm double bed, making love and then sleeping cuddled together, limbs entwined, off and on throughout the night.

Each morning Pamela would prepare breakfast which they would share, still warm and naked in her bed, propped up on the pillows, bare thighs touching. One morning, towards the end of this idyll, Miss Gray turned to her young companion and asked: "Tell me Julia, darling, are you still a virgin?"

Still quite unused to such frankness, Julia coloured a little and stammered her reply,

"Er, well, no, not really, I suppose."

"Come now, my dear, you are or you aren't. Have you slept with a man yet?"

"Well there was this boy, last Summer. At a party actually. But we didn't even get undressed properly. I just took off my pants and he was groping my titties under my blouse. It was all rather unsatisfactory. More of a fumble in the dark ..."

"Yes, one needs a considerate and experienced lover to make those first encounters worthwhile!" Miss Gray mused aloud. An idle hand strayed to cup Julia's soft, round breast and tweaked at the relaxed nipple to send a shiver down the young girl's spine.

"I was fortunate at your age," Pamela Gray continued, "to have a most considerate older man as my first lover. He took great pains to be gentle and to ensure my pleasure. In my turn I learned avidly what was needed to pleasure him and he, of course, proved to be an excellent teacher. So, then let us agree that you are - how shall we say? - a demi-vierge: breached but as yet unsatisfied. Do you think it would add pleasantly to your stock of experience to make love with the sort of mature man I have described?"

The conversation was becoming very intriguing in a way that touched Julia very personally. She cuddled up to her lover, throwing an arm across her svelte tummy and nestling her head against her breasts. Julia's lips nuzzled at the tender flesh and her mouth suckled a flaccid teat.

"Sounds fascinating," she said, releasing the already stiffening nipple from between her lips.

Pamela returned the embrace. Passing an arm around the bare shoulders of her companion, she continued, "You may be surprised to learn, my dear, that even today I am fortunate enough to have a lover - a male lover I mean - who is every bit as considerate and worldly wise as the dear man who first showed me the mutual joy to be had between a man and a woman."

Julia was indeed surprised. It is a trait of the young only to think of friends and lovers in the context which most nearly touches them. Julia had never so much as considered Miss Gray as having relationships outside the school and beyond 'The Sisters'.

"My proposal, then," Pamela Gray went on climactically, "is that we should invite my man-friend to take you to bed and to initiate you in the pleasures of sex between a man and a woman. In short, I am offering to share him with you."

Julia gave a whoop of delight. "Oh what a perfectly gorgeous idea. You are such a wonderful darling, dearest Pamela." And she flung her arms about her friend and kissed her full on the mouth, their breasts crushing together nipple to nipple.

Recovering from this frenzy of delight Pamela Gray agreed to make the necessary arrangements for that same night, remarking that it would be a small Christmas present for both her loves.

"And now I think you can show me how grateful you are," she smiled as Julia's hand crept between her thighs.

It needed only a telephone call to arrange for Miss Gray's mysterious man friend to visit School House that very same evening. Still in her role of elder sister, Pamela supervised Julia's preparations, assisting her with her maquillage and lending her a subtle Givenchy perfume which the young woman carefully applied between her breasts and at other yet more intimate places. By the time Pamela was satisfied, Julia had been transformed from an attractive schoolgirl into an elegantly lovely young woman.

The proceeds of their recent shopping trip to Edinburgh also came in useful. To welcome their guest Julia wore a cream silk blouse and a matching woollen skirt which swirled loosely about her calves. A wide leather belt emphasised her slender waist. This pale outfit set off to perfection the rich, shining auburn of her hair which tumbled loosely over her shoulders.

Beneath the blouse, on Pamela's advice, Julia wore no bra. "Your firm young breasts need no artificial support, darling girl. And the silk will feel so good on your bare flesh," the headmistress had remarked. Under her skirt Julia wore totally feminine french knickers extravagantly frilled in cream silk and white stockings held taut by delicately frilled garters.

Promptly, at the appointed time, a little after dinner, a ring came at the door - their guest had arrived. Pamela hastened to let him in and stood clasping his arm while an amused smile played about her lips at Julia's astonishment.

"I am sure you know my friend Hugh quite well already," she said by way of introduction.

Of course Julia knew Hugh McFee. As the only presentable male who regularly visited the school, the art master was the centre of intrigue and speculation among all the girls. Certainly, he was the object of many schoolgirl crushes both overt and unspoken. From time to time the idle chatter in the dormitory had turned to consideration of his private life. Was he married? What about girl friends? Never, though, had he been mentioned in connection with Miss Gray.

The three of them, after Julia had overcome her surprise, settled themselves comfortably in the living room. Pamela produced a bottle of wine, an excellent Marques D Murietta rioja, and handed round glasses. Julia savoured the delicate aroma and the oaky bite of the wine in her mouth and relaxed as the usual chatter of greeting and social 'feeling out' went on.

"So, are you content with my choice of man for you?" Pamela remarked after a while.

In fact Julia could not have been better pleased! Although she was not one of those who had developed a crush on the craggily built art master, she was certainly among those who had rated him a very attractive man.

"Oh yes, dear Pamela. Yes indeed! He couldn't be more perfect," beamed a delighted and highly excited Julia.

"Well, I think it would be most to your liking if you enjoyed your first taste of Hugh without an audience - just a deux. Am I right?"

"I should prefer it - if you don't mind, darling."

"Of course not. Off you both go and mind you enjoy yourselves," Pamela smiled.

Hugh took Julia by the hand and led her into the bedroom, pushing the door shut behind them. The bedside light had already been dimmed in readiness and now a soft and sensual semi-darkness enveloped them. Hugh smiled down at her, his arms around her shoulders, as Julia lifted her face and offered him her mouth, moist lips slightly parted. They kissed deeply, Hugh's tongue probing between her lips, their tongues sucking greedily.

As the kiss broke and her head cleared from the erotic whirl it had induced, Julia became aware of Hugh's fingers, busy at the buttons of her blouse. He parted the batiste material, thrusting his hands inside and pushing the garment over Julia's shoulders. With a helpful shrug of her shoulders she let the blouse slip from her and stood naked to the waist.

Hugh's firm but gentle hands caressed her bare skin with an easy sensuality. Stroking over her shoulders, cupping her breasts and squeezing the pliant flesh tenderly, then continuing to mould her waist and draw her to him. He bent his head and briefly rasped his tongue over her teats, leaving a damp trail on the sensitive skin of each aureole.

Julia sighed a sigh of complete happiness and again sought Hugh's mouth with her own. Their lips nibbled at each other and tongues lapped as Hugh continued to release Julia from her clothing. The leather belt was undone and, soon after, the heavy woollen skirt slipped down her legs to pool at her feet.

Hugh's hands slipped under the waistband of her knickers and cupped firm buttock flesh. He kneaded her bum tenderly, pulling her against him so that her pubic mound ground against his own hardening manhood. Gradually the silken knickers were worked over the soft mounds of her bottom to bunch around Julia's upper thighs.

"Lie down on the bed Julia and make yourself comfortable while I get out of these things," he whispered against her ear.

Obediently Julia slipped off her knickers and lay naked but for her stockings on the bed she had so recently shared with Pamela Gray. Leaning on one elbow she turned to watch with avid interest as Hugh McFee stripped himself to reveal a well muscled torso which was lightly sprinkled with sandy curls. Julia gasped softly as his fully erect manhood popped into sight when he lowered his pants.

Naked now, he came to her and knelt beside her on the bed, offering himself to her to inspect.

Julia, as if in a dream, reached out and tenderly cupped his scrotum, feeling the weight of the balls within and gently stroking the wrinkled skin of the pouch. Dreamily she tangled her fingers in his pubic thatch enjoying the pleasant coarseness of the hairs. Lightly she clasped the shaft, sensing its power as she ran her fingers over the veins and the soft skin.

Holding him now with both hands, feeling him twitch involuntarily under her touch, she drew the skin back from the crown and exposed the crimson dome of flesh up to the glans. A small bead of oily moisture gathered at the tip. With a slender finger she caught it and smeared it over the crown to make it shine slickly.

Tentatively she put out her tongue and lowering her head, licked at the suave flesh, tasting a man's salty taste for the first time. Boldness and her liking for this sport both increasing, she played her tongue rapidly over Hugh's manhood and forming her lips into an 'O' she finally took him into her mouth.

Very gently Hugh withdrew from her mouth and lay down beside her.

"More of that later, darling Julia. Now let me pleasure you," and he kissed her softly on the mouth.

Only too willingly Julia lay back and gave herself up to the thrilling sensations Hugh now wrought in her body.

Again he bent his head to her breasts, his moist tongue lapping over the aureolae. Then he was drawing gobbets of sweet flesh into his mouth, suckling on her teats as the nipples sprang erect with excitement. Sucking hard he brought his teeth into play to nip gently at the hardening nubs. Julia groaned with deep pleasure and clasped him to her as she wriggled and squirmed with delight.

Leaving her well used breasts he drew his mouth down Julia's belly leaving a trail of wetness on the smooth, milky flesh. His mouth open he sucked at her Mount of Venus and his tongue probed the lips that nestled beneath the auburn curls.

Then his hands were on her thighs, parting her legs and caressing the damp inner flesh. Gradually his hands crept nearer to her womanhood until his fingers probed between her nether lips. The intensity of the feelings his stroking engendered in her loins grew unabated. Julia was almost out of her mind with lust, nothing existed for her but those lovely feelings that rippled through her.

His fingers were inside her now, paddling in her freely flowing juices. Hugh worked his fingers deep in her orifice, gently frigging her, smearing her thighs with her spending. He found her clitoris and tenderly massaged the tiny nodule before bending his head to lick softly at the erect bundle of nerve ends. Julia was in a state of rapture, writhing and groaning pleasurably under his subtle, sure touch.

Then his face was above hers, looking down and smiling,

"I think you are ready now, Julia."

"Oh yes. Yes, I'm ready. Please put your lovely cock in me. Fuck me, fuck me now."

She opened her thighs wide and drew her feet up towards her. Hugh kneeling between her legs, taking his erection in one hand, placed it at the porch of her womanhood and slowly eased the crown into her drooling quim.

At the slight pain of this first intrusion Julia winced and gave a soft cry. Hugh waited until, with a smile, Julia urged him on and he, with a steady smoothness, thrust into her liquid sex until he was fully inside her. For long seconds he held himself motionless within her, filling her with his meaty rod.

It was so good! So very good! To feel his male hardness inside her, filling her up. To clasp the welcome intruder in her damp womanhood. To feel his warm bulk upon her, his belly on hers, her breasts coolly spreading on his chest. To smell his male smells mingled with his cologne.

He began to move inside her. Slowly at first, then with more vigour, the muscles of her sex clasping at him as he withdrew and then reentered her.

Gradually the climax built in her. At each thrilling spasm, Julia breathed 'Oooh!' between her teeth. Her feet locked over his calves, her hands reached over his buttocks to draw him even deeper inside her. The sensations in her sex and flowing through her body like a torrent of sexual electricity became overwhelming. Her fingers dug into his flesh, her feet drummed on the bed. Then she was yelling, celebrating her climax in a long drawn out wail as her orgasm flooded her senses, blotting out the rest of the world.

Still Hugh pistoned his erection in her clutching, sopping wet sex. Urgently Julia whispered: "Please, oh please, come in me. Fill me with your come. Ungh, please, unff, oh please ..."

His buttocks tightened and again he was motionless inside her, his bulk pressing her flat to the bed, flesh melding with flesh. His cock pulsed and his seed erupted from him splashing into her in a continuous stream.

After, they clung together panting. Hugh's cock deflated inside her and slipped from between the lips of her sex drawing a trail of stickiness over her thigh. Gently he kissed her mouth and her eyelids. Julia sweetly smiled her thanks and curled on his chest. So they lay, limbs entwined, happily sated, when Pamela's voice broke softly upon their reverie,

"May I join you now?"

She stood beside the bed in the half-light, palely naked. In one hand she carried three glasses and in the other yet another bottle of well chilled wine.

"Oh yes, dearest Pamela. Hugh is absolutely gorgeous. Please do let us share him now," Julia responded with girlish enthusiasm.

And so Miss Gray climbed onto the bed beside her companions. For a while they sat propped on pillows, Hugh sandwiched between the two females, sipping wine and chatting bawdily. From time to time a kiss would be exchanged , a breast or male member idly fondled.

Soon it became obvious from the attention that he began to pay to their abundant charms and from the twitching of his penis under their hands that Hugh was fully recovered from his bout with Julia and had completely recruited his forces. Pamela straddled his broad chest and leaning forward dangled her heavy breasts over his face. Hugh reached up to take a heavy cantaloupe in each hand and began to knead the pliant, milky flesh. Pamela moaned her approval throatily, and frotted herself against his chest the while.

Hugh increased the pressure of his grip on Pamela's rich flesh, drawing the flesh into cones and pinching and rolling the swelling nipples between his fingers. He mouthed one teat then the other, drawing the rosy pink crown into his mouth, tonguing it firmly against his palate and sucking hard.

Pamela, her engorged and fiercely throbbing teats wet with her lover's saliva, slid along his body, caressing his skin with hers, until her face was level with his stiffening weapon. Steadying it with one hand, she licked it thoroughly, tasting the musky savour left on the rod of flesh by Julia's sex. She concentrated her attentions about the dome and glans until the purple flesh was slickly wet. Then, forming an 'O' with her carmine lips she engulfed him completely, drawing the cock into her mouth until the stiff rod lodged in her throat.

Hugh was fully erect by now, hard and tumescent, throbbing on her tongue. Pamela sucked hard as she rode her mouth up and down the entire length of the fleshy shaft.

She released him, letting the cock slip from her lips with a slight 'plop', and with a glance invited Julia to take her place. Eagerly the younger woman supplanted her friend and, herself supporting Hugh's full erection in one hand, licked avidly along its length, tasting, as she did so, the salty savour of Hugh's flesh commingled with the musky taste of her own juices and Pamela's saliva. Tentatively she again took the crown between her lips and gradually began to work the whole length into her gaping jaws. It felt huge but wonderful; overpowering and delicious. She felt her jaws must crack. She gagged as the tip finally touched the back of her

throat. Nevertheless, she persevered and soon was sucking and tonguing the pulsing member as if it were the
most delicious sweetmeat.

Hugh, while greatly enjoying Julia and Pamela's joint
ministrations, was not idle. His hands crept between
both the young women's thighs, finding their moist sexes
and treating them both to a vigorous frigging.

Pamela whispered an instruction in Julia's ear and
she, a little reluctantly, released the juicy titbit from
between her lips. Pamela straddled Hugh's hips and
opening her pussy lips, impaled herself on his uprearing
organ, exhaling a deep sigh of enjoyment. Sinuously
she began to move her hips, working Hugh's weapon
inside her, a blissful smile on her face.

Julia placed herself over Hugh's face and offered
her hungry womanhood to his mouth. His tongue lapped
over her labiae and plunged into her liquid sex. Thus
Pamela rode her lover's tool to bliss, climaxes breaking
over her in great tidal waves of happiness as Julia
fondled her breasts and bent to suck at her lips. Julia
too was brought to orgasm by Hugh's mouth and tongue,
screaming as she ground her musky snatch into his face.

Sweating, delirious with joy, the two girls exchanged
places. Once more Julia felt herself breached by Hugh's
delicious male hardness, the pole of flesh stretching her
wide, the tip seeming to invade the very mouth of her
womb. Again the two women rode their lover to ultimate release then, their skin glistening with the sweat
of their exertions, slipped from his body to lay panting
beside him.

The edge of Hugh's appetite had been dulled a little
during his earlier bout of lovemaking with Julia and so

he had been able to hold himself in check as he pleasured his two female companions to the full. Now in urgent need of release he knelt above Pamela and gently stroked his shaft as it jutted eagerly towards his reclining lover.

"Oh yes, darling, come over my tits, cover me with your lovely spunk," she urged him dreamily.

By way of encouragement she clasped her breasts together, kneading the soft mounds. Hugh straddled her and pushed his tool into the yielding channel between her creamy bubbies, smearing the titflesh with her own juices and those of Julia too. Vigorously he pounded his rampant male organ at her elastic flesh while she clasped the soft orbs about him. Soon his reserves of control were totally exhausted and his seed churned within him. He reared up, stroking his throbbing engine and lanced spurts of warm, creamy jism over Pamela's breasts. Jet after jet of his warm effusion followed, splashing over her body, covering her from chest to belly.

Languidly Pamela dabbled her fingers in the gooey liquid that clung to her skin. She held out her hand to Julia, inviting her to lap Hugh's seed from her fingers. Julia consumed the proffered morsel, relishing its saltiness, then thirsty for more she lapped at her lover's defiled skin until she was clean.

Thus through the night they pleasured each other, giving and receiving generously. Between bouts of frenzied sex they dozed fitfully, curled in each others' arms and towards dawn, completely exhausted, fell into a deep sleep.

Worn out by their lovemaking the happy trio slept late and awoke near midday. As was her custom, Pamela prepared breakfast and the three of them partook ravenously of toast and scrambled eggs, still cosy and naked in Pamela's large, soft bed.

Julia, with the resilience of youth, had fully recovered from the depredations of the previous night of debauchery. Randy again and anxious to have Hugh's attention focused on her, she sought to turn their thoughts down a bawdy path. With a cheeky grin she asked,

"Tell me, Pamela, does Hugh ever use the paddle on you?"

"But of course he does," Pamela responded with a smile. "There's nothing quite so stimulating between lovers as a little loving spanking. Why do you ask?"

"I thought that since he had given me so much pleasure - if he enjoyed that sort of thing - Hugh might like to spank my bottom," Julia replied archly.

"My darling little minx. Can you doubt but that Hugh would jump at the chance of spanking your sweet little rump? You are a dear girl for suggesting it," and Pamela exchanged a glance with Hugh who smiled broadly in anticipation of the treat to come.

The breakfast things were quickly put to one side. Hugh got up and padded, naked, across the room to settle himself on a plain wooden chair that stood in one corner. In the clear light of a December mid-morning Julia now had the opportunity to get a good look at him, to admire his creamy skin, lightly covered in sandy hair and to appreciate his compact bum and, of course, his thick endowment now lazily at rest amidst the coarse pubic nest.

"Come here Julia and lie over my lap," he commanded somewhat sharply.

During the night's activities Julia had managed to lose her stockings and so she too was stark naked as she crossed the floor and obediently draped herself across Hugh's lap. She braced herself almost on tip-toe, her hands flat on the floor and pushing her bottom up towards him. She felt his manhood twitch against her belly and cheekily ground her flesh down on his, enjoying the tickle of his hairs on her abdomen and the obvious effect her body had on the man's senses.

'Craaak!' his hand landed squarely on the fullest flesh of Julia's behind. Julia squealed and jerked involuntarily. Steadily the spanking progressed as Hugh's heavy hand smote his victim's jiggling nates, quivering the ripe flesh.

It hurt, of course. But only just enough pain to make things interesting and to give emphasis to the overwhelming sensation of being dominated and controlled that thrilled Julia and quickened her pulse.

Hugh hooked a leg over her calves and pushed down on her back thus holding her rigid while his free hand continued to pummel her rump. Julia yelled freely and wriggled against him in a mock serious effort to avoid his hand. But above all, the beautiful, tummy churning excitement was building in her all the time.

At last, her bottom stinging and blushing hotly, Hugh was finished. His penis had now reached the full tumescence of erection and burrowed urgently into the soft swell of her belly. Julia too was hot and ready, her sex drooling expectantly. Lazily Hugh's hand passed over her burning bum-flesh, luxuriating in the plump amplitude of her well rounded nates.

"Stand up!" he ordered, releasing his grip on her as he himself stood to face her, his eyes - harsher now it seemed - catching and holding her gaze.

"Aren't you forgetting your manners? Isn't it customary to thank your master for punishment?"

Julia, a little surprised by the stern tone, soon entered into the spirit.

"Yes, er, sorry. Thank you Hugh for spanking my bum."

"Sir! You must call me sir!" he enjoined gruffly.

"Sorry sir. Thank you sir!"

"And does it sting as it should, my girl?" and he reached out to take her breasts, one in each hand.

"Ooh yes, sir. My poor bottom's throbbing terribly."

He was kneading her flesh now, squeezing the youthful breasts, squeezing them harder, harder. This treatment, so assertive, contrasted with his gentleness of the night before. Julia, however, felt herself responding - this new firmness was oh so exciting. She licked her lips, still gazing into his eyes.

His fingers worked over her breasts which were now firm and swollen with anticipation and found her erect, stiff nipples. Gently at first, then with increasing intensity, he rolled the rosy ripe teats between his fingers. Then he was squeezing, harder, harder. Julia closed her eyes and groaned deeply. Still working her tit-flesh, Hugh spoke: "Now I suppose you want me to fuck you, you horny little bitch?"

"Oh yesss! Yes, please. Fuck me please," Julia groaned thickly.

188

"Get on the bed, on all fours. Straddle Pamela. Your bum towards the end."

Quickly, obediently, Julia complied, arranging herself atop her female lover who reclined beneath her. In this position the two girls could kiss and Pamela busied herself with her protege's engorged tit-flesh.

Hugh paddled his forefinger in Julia's juicy quim then, parting her still throbbing bum cheeks, he plunged the lubricated digit into her anus, wriggling it within her fundament. Julia gasped at this new and unexpected intrusion but then let a broad grin of contentment spread over her lips.

Hugh mounted her then, thrusting his cock inside her slavering womanhood, and began to roger her. Divinely filled in both her nether holes, already brought to a fever pitch by the spanking and the strangely exciting dominance Hugh now exercised, Julia came off almost instantly. Orgasm followed orgasm as Hugh continued to pound his organ inside her, reaming her pussy and almost threatening to split her in two with the power of his thrusts.

At last, however, he was coming too. Quickly withdrawing from her he jetted his divinely gooey seed over Pamela's belly as she lay beneath them. Pamela for her part sighed her appreciation and drew Julia down upon her to cover her body too with their lover's creamy tribute.

Later they all shared the bath, taking it in turns to soak in the warm soapy waters while the others lathered and rinsed their well pleasured flesh.

A day or so later Pamela drove Julia, somewhat regretfully, to the airport to catch her flight. Their pleasant interlude was ended. Julia for her part, while looking forward to a New York Christmas with keen anticipation, unlike many schoolgirls was really looking forward to the new term when again she could pick up the threads of an intimate education that was very much to her taste.

Elliot was on the telephone when Susan brought him his pre-lunch cocktail. He was perched on the corner of his dark wood writing desk, his weight on one foot which was planted squarely on the floor while his other leg swung idly back and forth as he talked. He gave Susan a stern look over the mouthpiece as if to warn her to mind her own business and carried on with his conversation.

Susan was much too preoccupied to fall victim to natural, female curiosity. She really hoped that she had prepared the cocktail to her husband's liking and was concentrating hard on placing it just as he liked, just so, on the side table by his armchair. Elliot was very particular in his requirements and kept Susan up to a very exacting standard. If there should be any shortcomings there would be hell to pay.

Carefully Susan placed the small silver tray on which she had carried the single glass of dry martini - straight up, with an olive - in the exact centre of the low, leather topped table. The herbie scent of the cocktail tickled her nose, the chilled glass was frosted with condensation.

Susan had remembered to dip down, bending at the knee, to place the tray on the table top. She straightened up, breathing a silent sigh of relief that nothing had spilled or had been upset. She was often so clumsy, or so Elliot was always telling her. She paused to smooth her skirt. Elliot was still talking in a low murmur and, without meaning to, she caught herself listening.

"Very well, Jack, that's agreed. She'll be with you tomorrow. Arriving by the eleven o'clock train. No, no, she'll take a taxi from the station. Don't want to spoil her."

The handset clicked back onto its rest breaking the connection. The sound recalled Susan to herself and to what she had been doing. Elliot was looking at her with his steady blue eyed gaze. When he spoke his tone betrayed mild annoyance, as though admonishing an habitually wayward child that had been caught out in some minor transgression.

"Well Susan, since you insist on eavesdropping I may as well satisfy your curiosity. That telephone call concerned you anyway.

"I've sometimes thought that you might benefit from - how shall I put it? Yes. A change of scene. A fresh hand on the reins. Since I shall be going abroad for a couple of weeks, now seems to be an opportune time.

"I've arranged for you to stay with a friend of mine, Mr Frost. I think he will do you good. A much firmer chap altogether , not forgiving or indulgent like myself. Yes, you will benefit from firm handling."

All of this was quite a surprise to poor Susan. She had had no inkling of her husband's planned overseas trip, no more than she had of his plans for her temporary disposal. She had entered Elliot's study hoping to escape the comparatively mild upbraiding that any small failure to meet her husband's standards of behaviour and decorum might have earned her before she was allowed to retreat to her kitchen and now she found herself about to be placed in the hands of the unknown Mr Frost who must be a veritable tyrant. She was quite dumbstruck, standing rooted to the spot. Naturally there would be no arguing with Elliot's decision. She would, as always, do precisely what she was told.

Elliot was consulting his watch, a handsome half-hunter fob watch which he cradled in the palm of his hand.

"Hmmm, I see that there's about an hour before lunch. Ample time to remind you that listening to other people's conversations is not acceptable behaviour. Get yourself ready."

With a look of solemn resignation on her face, Susan fetched the cane from its place in the corner and handed it to her husband. She bent over the desk and reaching down, flipped her loose skirt up over her back to reveal plumply rounded bare buttocks. Her eyes clenched tightly shut against the anticipated onslaught, she reached across to grasp the far edge of the desk.

The next morning, early, a taxi arrived to take Susan to the station. Elliot helped her into the back seat along with the small suitcase that contained the few essential items he had picked out for her to take along for her stay with his friend. Elliot had also closely supervised her personal preparations for the journey, selecting her outfit and making sure she brushed her rich, shoulder length, chestnut hair until it shone in the early morning sunlight. As a parting gesture he placed in her hand a plain brown envelope addressed to Mr Frost. With hardly a glance at it, Susan placed it in her slim handbag along with her train ticket, her handkerchief and the small amount of money Elliot had given her against 'emergencies' on the journey.

At the station Susan found her reserved seat in a corner of a first class compartment. She placed her suitcase in the rack overhead and took her seat. She sat perfectly erect, heels and knees together, back straight, head up, her chin slightly tilted, her hands folded almost primly in her lap before her. She adopted this position quite naturally and without thinking, thanks to many hours of Elliot's assiduous posture training.

As the train gathered speed and the busy clusters of working class houses that spread themselves around the railway were replaced by rolling green fields, Susan stared impassively out of the window. When the train stopped at intermediate stations she barely seemed to notice, hardly acknowledging the coming or going of fellow passengers who shared her compartment temporarily.

As the journey progressed there was nothing in her outwardly calm demeanour to betray the increasing feeling of apprehension that seized upon her. There was only the emptiness in her tummy, a general quickening of her pulse and heartbeat, a sense of breathlessness and the teeming thoughts that thronged her mind. Susan had a fair idea of what might be in store for her during her stay at Mr Frost's house. He and Elliot were quite obviously colleagues of like mind and interests and she had garnered plenty of experience at her husband's hands. Nevertheless, despite her worst imaginings, the thought of disobedience, of not placing herself in the hands of her husband's friend and her new, albeit temporary, mentor never entered her head.

When she caught sight of the name of her destination as the train slowed and drew to a halt at a quiet country station, Susan climbed down from the carriage onto the deserted platform. In a lane outside she found a taxi and showed the driver the address that Elliot had thoughtfully written out for her on a slip of paper. A few minutes drive through the quiet countryside brought her to the edge of a sizable village where the taxi drew up outside a substantial red brick Victorian house. It was an imposing structure of the type which in a town would, by now, have been broken up into flats or worse into pokey bed-sitting rooms. In this case, though, the house remained as originally intended, a capacious family home, with quarters for servants in its attic rooms, set back from the road in a tranquil and well tended garden.

Paying for the taxi took most of the small amount of money Elliot had allowed her. Susan took up her suitcase, clutched her handbag under her other arm and with some not inconsiderable trepidation set off up the shingle drive to the front door.

The man who opened the door in answer to her ring was nothing like the dreadful ogre she had conjured up in her troubled imagination. Mr Frost was nondescript - a short, middle-aged man, his sandy hair receding, a tweed sports- coat flapping unbuttoned over a burgeoning paunch.

This comforting and ultimately misleading first impression was soon dispelled when Susan found herself, a few minutes later, facing him across his desk in a study which was quite similar to the one in which so many trying interviews with Elliot had taken place back at home. Frost treated her to a long and thorough appraisal without offering a word. The round lenses of his wire-framed spectacles reflected the sunlight that streamed through the half opened window, making it impossible for her to see his eyes or to gain any impression of what he might be thinking. Faced with this unnerving blankness Susan became increasingly unsettled as she stood in the enveloping and heavy silence. She shifted her weight nervously from one leg to another and fought hard to stop her eyes wandering about the room.

Frost was enjoying the view from where he sat behind the desk. He made a mental inventory of the charms of the young woman who stood before him, from her delightful, heart shaped face which betrayed a pleasing air of innocence, mainly due to her wide, brown, doe-like eyes, right down to her patent leather shod feet. She certainly had a fine figure from what he could tell. The grey designer jacket with a crisp white blouse beneath, the pencil skirt just brushing above the knees set off her charms very well indeed. She was well-fleshed - buxom Elliot had called her. Frost noted the swell of her bosom under the tightly buttoned jacket and her plump calves webbed in black nylon. She was ripely attractive now, just at the pitch of sweet, toothsome perfection, Frost thought to himself, but Elliot would have to be strict with her to make sure she stayed in good shape. Frost permitted himself a thin-lipped smile, Elliot would doubtless enjoy doing just that.

Frost opened the envelope that Susan had given to him as she stood on his doorstep. He scanned the closely written sheet of foolscap that it contained, glancing up occasionally to look again at his delightful new charge.

"For pity's sake stand still and stop fidgeting about. Stop slouching and stand up straight."

Susan had automatically assumed the penitential posture, her head slightly inclined, her hands clasped before her while she stood waiting on Mr Frost's pleasure. At his word of command she drew herself erect and stood rigidly to attention while clasping each elbow with the opposing hand behind her back. Frost was pleased to note that in this position the young woman's bosom was thrust out even more prominently.

"Do you know what is in this letter?"

"No sir."

"Just so. I think we can dispose with formality although I am pleased that Elliot has managed to inculcate some elements of politeness in your behaviour. You may call me Uncle Jack."

"Thank you sir, er, er, Uncle Jack."

"Now, be quiet and I shall read to you what your husband, or is it your master, has to say on your behalf."

Frost returned to the crisp sheet of white paper in his hand. He scanned over the opening remarks which described Susan's daily routine, her diet and so on, mumbling the words softly to himself in an undertone before he spoke out aloud.

"Ah yes, here we are. Pay attention: 'Susan has been rigorously trained to a very high standard. She still, unhappily, displays a tendency to laziness and can be careless. From time to time she is insolent and I have had to punish her for this quite severely. Perhaps you could give these areas of her development some attention.

"'While she is with you please treat her as your own property. I have outlined her usual daily routine and penalties but please feel free to vary this as you see fit.

"'As you can now see, she has a fine, full figure of which I am very proud. Her breasts, in particular, are ripe and round but despite their fullness they are firm and pert - well able to stand out for themselves without the artificial aid of a bra. They are also very sensitive, both to pleasant and to painful stimuli. I mention this last fact as I know that this area of the female anatomy is of especial interest and delight to you.'"

Susan felt a hot flush of embarrassment creep over her. It was just as if Elliot were there in the room, parading her naked before a perfect stranger and discussing intimate details of her physique with him. Then a quiver of dread, stark and chill replaced the heat of shame as the full import of the words that had been read out dawned upon her.

Mr Frost was refolding the letter and replacing it with fussy neatness into the thin brown envelope. He spoke again,

"Well, young lady, there's no point in further pleasantries and introductions. We had better get on. Leave your case here and follow me."

Susan, trained to obedience, allowed him to lead her from the room. She followed him along a passageway that lead to the back of the house and down a stairway that evidently lead into a basement. At the bottom, he operated a lock and pushed open a heavy door. A light switch clicked and the room was flooded with harsh white light as he handed Susan into the room.

"Get yourself ready. I shall be back directly."

And he was gone, the thick, leather covered, metal studded door thumping shut behind him as if sealing the entrance to a tomb.

Susan was confused. She knew what Elliot would expect of her but this stranger might be different. She understood perfectly that in these cases detail was all and that inattention to such detail could only increase the severity of what was to happen to her thereafter. Did Mr Frost want her naked or just stripped to her underwear? With shoes or barefoot?

She had to do something so she slipped off her high-heeled court shoes and placed them neatly side by side. Standing in stockinged feet she unbuttoned her jacket and took it off, likewise she unzipped the tight skirt and sloughed it down her legs. There was a chair, an ordinary wooden kitchen chair, just by where she was standing. Susan folded the jacket and skirt carefully and laid them on the seat. She unbuttoned her blouse and draped that over the back of the chair.

The air in the basement room was chilly. Susan hugged her arms about herself, feeling the gooseflesh erupt on her bare skin.

Now that she had a chance to examine her surroundings a different chill seized her - a chill of terror as she realised that the basement room had been set up as a sort of dungeon or torture chamber.

A bare, unshaded lamp, fixed high in the ceiling poured hard, clinical light down upon everything. The walls were grey-washed and blank. If there had ever been any windows these had been bricked up and all trace of them assiduously effaced. A grille of steel bars stretched from wall to wall at one end of the room to partition off a portion of the space to form a cell. Behind the bars Susan could make out the crude and basic furnishings - a rough wooden bench, a bucket and a china basin and ewer in a stand.

Horrified, Susan continued to look about her. She shuddered when she glimpsed the array of whips, crops, canes and other implements of correction that were neatly arranged around the walls. Close by she noted a raised platform, covered with a dark cloth, just wide enough for a victim to lie or kneel upon to undergo punishment. Arching above this elongated dais was a forbidding arrangement of steel bars and pulleys from which depended several sets of manacles and sturdy chains. Elsewhere in the room she noted other systems of restraint and chastisement, some of which were all too familiar to her while there were others the exact use of which she could only guess at.

She hugged herself tighter, trembling and wishing fervently that Elliot would never take it into his head to convert the basement of their own home into a similarly loathsome chamber.

The sound of the door opening and closing roused her. Mr Frost had returned. He had changed out of the tweed sports jacket and grey flannels and now wore a black kimono-like robe, loosely cut to allow him freedom of movement against the vigorous exercise that was to come. When he saw Susan his face took on a look of distinct displeasure.

"I thought I had told you to get yourself ready. Why are you still half dressed. Is this wilful disobedience?"

Susan, without thinking, began to blurt out her excuses:

"But you didn't tell me what ..."

Frost's open palm cracked smartly across her cheek, damming the flow of her nervous babble and reminding Susan of her situation. Frost's face wore a purse lipped look of contempt as he spoke,

"I do not wish to hear your excuses. Is this an example of your insolence? Disobedient and insolent! I can see that we shall have to work hard with you. Now get undressed properly."

Susan reached behind her and unclasped the bra. She shrugged it from her shoulders, spilling her ample breasts from the constraining cups. Likewise she hooked thumbs in the waistband of her panties and shucked them off. A curt gesture from Mr Frost stopped her there and she stood to attention awaiting his further instructions.

Frost treated her to a long drawn out scrutiny as he enjoyed the sight of her ample figure displayed for his express gratification. The wasp-waist corset that cinched her midriff and from which depended long elastic suspenders to hold taut the sheer black stockings made her seem even more lewdly naked than having her strip completely. He decided that there would be plenty of time to admire her completely naked as she went about her chores in the days to come. For now this erotic half-nudity was perhaps even more gratifying.

Elliot had been quite right about her breasts. The heavy gourds of flesh jutted proudly from the girl's chest, massy but firm. The nipples, still crinkled and flaccid from their confinement in the tight bra still slept on the rich mound of ivory flesh. Her shoulders, throat and the upper slopes of her bust were liberally sprinkled with delicious butter gold freckles. A soft pink hue of embarrassment which now crept over her cheeks, throat and bosom only lent further charm to the sight.

Frost cradled one sac on his open palm and felt the flesh yield pliantly as it overflowed his grasp. His thumb caressed the nipple which awoke to stiffen to a hard, brown acorn.

"Hmmm. Not yet pierced. Maybe we can attend to that while you are staying with me."

A knot of anguish unravelled in Susan's stomach. She hated needles, feared them with a phobic terror. The very thought of a thin, cold shaft of steel piercing her tender flesh as, doubtless, she was made to watch, wrung her bowels with panic.

"Hands on your head. Stand up straight!"

Susan adopted the required position which had the effect of poising her bosom even more proudly on her ribcage.

Frost noted with approval that Elliot kept her smoothly shaven everywhere except at her pubic region where a rich crop of chestnut curls erupted at the vee of her closely pressed thighs.

Frost slapped Susan's plump right breast with his open palm. The blow was nicely judged to sting intensely and then leave a dull ache in the tender flesh. A well judged flick of the fingertips after the flat of the hand had connected with yielding flesh served to further intensify the discomfort.

Susan's plump tits rocked from side to side under the impact. She gasped with shock as the realisation of the pain hit her and her face contorted in a grimace of anguish.

Frost slapped the left breast, rocking the ripe pods back in the opposite direction. Susan whimpered and the trace of a tear stood at the corner of her eye, then repeated the process, slapping first the right breast then the left. This time the intensity of the pain forced a cry of anguish from Susan's lips,

"Owwch! Oh shit!"

Frost glared at her.

"Does you master allow such language when you are being punished?"

"No, no he doesn't ... Uncle Jack."

"Then kindly hold your tongue."

Frost resumed where he had left off and Susan braced herself to suffer in silence as he slapped each breast in turn, first the right then the left, quivering the sweetly rounded pods of flesh.

When, after a few minutes of such treatment, he stopped, Susan's poor pained bosom was flushed an angry red. Tears of pain trickled over the unfortunate victim's cheeks as she bit hard on her lip to fight down the urge to whimper.

Beneath the nagging throb in her abused flesh, however, lurked a perverse subtext of erotic excitement. Her bosom was sore but her breasts were also swollen with lust. Her nipples were hard, fat, passion aroused buds. Not really surprising when one realised that despite her fear and loathing, which was genuine enough, Susan actually thrived on such treatment. In fact the more harshly she was chastised, the more bizarre and extreme the humiliation, the deeper her release when, and if, her tormentors allowed her the blessing of sexual climax.

"Jog on the spot," Frost commanded, his voice almost a whisper.

Susan thought she had misheard him and looked at him with a question in her eyes.

"Are you stupid? Or is this more of your insolence? I assume Elliot makes you exercise?"

Susan nodded her agreement. Exercise days with Elliot were arduous and exacting.

"Then I assume you know how to jog on the spot! So begin!"

Tentatively Susan began to jog, stepping on the spot, feeling the motion wobble her bosom to transmit sensations of discomfort through her frame.

"Faster. Put some effort into it. Get those legs up."

Susan increased the pace, raising her thighs to hip height. Her breasts bounced violently on her ribcage, the ripe fruit bounding madly in sympathy with the swaying of her torso.

Frost, a thin smile on his lips, enjoyed the sight for a few minutes before tearing himself away to rummage in one corner of the dungeon.

When he returned he signed to Susan with an abrupt gesture that she could stop her high-stepping exercise. He had brought with him a red plastic filing tray which, Susan saw, contained about a dozen shiny metal clips, rather like clothes pegs but made of stainless steel rather than wood.

Steadying her left breast with one hand, Frost selected a clip and worked the jaws over a fair sized gobbet of flesh. When the jaws snapped shut Susan could not help but gasp as the jolt of pain flashed through her.

Frost worked steadily to fix a pattern of pins around the surfaces of Susan's breasts. She squealed as the jaws bit into her pliant flesh, closing her eyes tightly and trying desperately not to flinch from her tormentor's touch.

Soon there remained just two clips lying in the cheap plastic tray. The rest hung from Susan's bosom, each weighty clip tugging at the pliant flesh to cause a continuous nagging throb to counterpoint the memory of the initial sharp pain when it had been set in place. It was only too obvious what Frost would do with the last two clips; Susan groaned inside. Sure enough, Frost plucked an engorged nipple between thumb and forefinger and snapped the clip in place. A red mist of pain clouded Susan's senses and she was barely aware of the second clip being fixed to her other nipple.

"Now again, jogging on the spot!" Frost's command penetrated the mist of pain.

Gingerly Susan began to step in obedience to his order. The clips jangled against each other as they tugged and pinched her flesh sending yet different and bitterly agonising sensations through poor Susan's body.

"Higher - get your knees higher!" Frost was implacable.

Susan could only obey and soon her breasts were bouncing maniacally against her ribcage while the clips bit fiercely into her flesh. Tears of anguish once again flowed down her cheeks and a soft mewling, keening rattled in her throat.

Just as Susan thought she could endure no more, Frost called a halt and removed the clips. Deep red pinch marks where the clips had bitten stood out in bitter contrast to the pink blush that the earlier spanking had raised. As the pain began to subside Susan, breathless from her efforts, offered up a silent sigh of relief.

But there was to be no respite for her. Frost had a whippy rattan cane in his hand. He flexed it before Susan's horrified gaze. Obedient to his murmured command she cupped her breasts, offering her bosom to the cruel bite of the cane.

The rattan swished in a great arc to crack over the smooth slope of Susan's uplifted bosom. Intense pain drove all other sense and sensation from her consciousness and she responded with a banshee howl. Again and again the cane struck home until warm, yielding flesh was stained with deep crimson stripes that threatened to coalesce into a single stain.

When the punishment ceased Susan became aware of Frost through her pain, ordering her to climb up onto the covered platform beneath the chain decked ironwork. She gritted her teeth and shook her head to clear it. At the back of her mind lingered the hope that this terrible man was about to change the focus of his operations. Surely, kneeling on all fours as he ordered, would invite his attention to her bottom and thus allow her bosom some respite. She climbed up onto the dais and arranged herself with her rump presented to Frost.

Frost ran his flattened palm appreciatively over the taut silken surface of her well fleshed rump. The girl's bottom was exquisite, beautifully rounded, fleshy and firm - it would respond to punishment magnificently. His finger probed between her thighs and dipped between the puffy, desire swollen lips of her sex. Frost nodded his satisfaction to himself. The girl was sopping wet, juices oozing from her. She might protest - and that was not unattractive - but deep down she was loving every humiliating, painful thing he was inflicting on her. He took his forefinger, lavishly slicked with her honey thick juices, and plunged it without ceremony into the tightness of Susan's anus. Her 'Unfff!' of enjoyment and the way the tight channel gripped on the welcome intruder told him all he needed to know.

Frost wiggled his finger briefly in her arse before unplugging abruptly. Beyond the range of her vision, Susan heard him rummaging about, then he was beside her and placing something on the platform beneath the arch of her torso. Sinking her head between her shoulders to look down towards her legs, Susan saw that, in fact, Frost had placed a rubber mat just beneath her plumply dangling breasts. It looked just like a pink rubber bath-mat, except that the surface was covered with a mass of hard rubber spikes.

Her curiosity aroused by this strange development, Susan, nevertheless, had to be content to wait for him to reveal his plans for her in his own time. Girls in her position were not invited to ask questions. She raised her head and straightened her back, bracing herself for the crack of wicked rattan across her trembling buttocks. But the expected blow did not come.

Susan could sense that Frost was still there. She could almost feel his gaze upon her, still appraising every inch of her pale, creamy nudity. Once or twice she could have sworn that she felt his cool breath on her back as he bent to sniff her woman smells or inspect her distended clitoris that poked impudently from her pussy lips, aroused despite her fear and discomfort. Still there was no swish as the cane cleaved the air, no crack as wood met and tormented reddening flesh.

Susan's shoulders began to feel stiff and her head sagged forward. Her arms, supporting the full weight of her torso, began to ache. The muscles in her forearms began to spasm. She tried to lock her elbows but it was no good. She began to droop lower, lower. It was then that the purpose of the strange, spike covered mat became clear to her.

The sore and tender pods of her breasts which dangled beneath her, brushed against the hard rubber spikes. It was as if a thousand hot needles had pricked her already irritated flesh. Susan jerked her body taut to raise her aching tit-flesh above this source of fresh pain. Her breasts were already swollen and tender from their earlier mistreatment, now they tingled hurtfully as echoes of yet deeper pain were reawakened.

'Thwaaak!' At last the cane cut across her backside. It was almost a relief to feel the throb in her arse cheeks which in its immediacy blotted out the nagging ache in her bosom. Again the cane cracked over her rump but with such force that Susan found herself pitched forward, her dangling teats brushing over the spikes beneath her.

Yet another cut of the cane and Susan found herself driven down hard onto the pad of spikes. Her breasts and bum were both pure agony. She couldn't control herself any more as the tears started again.

"Owwch! Ow - oh, please, no! No! No more. Please ...I b-b-beg!"

Frost seemed implacable. The cane cracked over Susan's jiggling rump thrice more while she babbled her pleas for mercy. Then a hand was thrust under her shoulders to ease her off of the bed of spikes and, to her relief, the rubber mat was removed from beneath her.

Frost's hands cupped both bruised tits and squeezed. It only needed the slightest pressure to transmit a paroxysm of hurt through the wounded flesh and set Susan whimpering piteously. With curt commands Frost again arranged his victim on the platform. He placed her hands behind her, hand clasping wrist in the small of her back. He drew down a length of chain from the overhead framework and fixed this to her wrists and forearms to manacle her limbs in position. Frost worked a pulley and accompanied by a clanking of chains, Susan felt her arms being pulled upwards, bracing her shoulders stiffly at attention and pitching her slightly forward to make her ruddy breasts dangle invitingly beneath her once more.

From his store of delights Frost produced a breast clamp, two jaws of leather lined wood connected at each end by a turnscrew. He fitted the contraption over poor Susan's swollen mammaries and turned down the screws until the jaws just held on the elastic flesh, the weight of the device pulling them down, distending the flesh.

Very slowly, a fraction of an inch at a time, he increased the pressure on the poor girl's tortured bosom. With each minute turn of the screw, Susan howled anew and her face contorted to a mask of anguish. Soon the plump gourds were squeezed to their limits, the flesh swollen and taut, the trapped fluids making the melons of flesh bulge beneath the wooden shackle, the skin becoming stretched and shiny. The nipples jutted on the taut stretched flesh like fat, ripe cherries, succulent to the point of bursting. Again Frost cupped each sphere to jolt shafts of agony through his victim's flesh before he finally released her.

"Hmm. Brave girl. You did well. Very sore are they?"

Gingerly, Susan cupped her abused flesh in a vain attempt to comfort herself. Yes, they were very sore, she nodded.

"Maybe we can soothe them a little."

In her naivete Susan thought that Frost was offering to fetch some comforting salve to ease the aches in her breasts. She was soon disabused of that notion when Frost opened his robe to show himself naked and healthily erect beneath and ordered her to kneel before him.

Susan knew what was expected then. So often similar sessions with Elliot had ended thus. She placed her hands behind her and put out her tongue to lap at Frost's weapon as he held the thick, pulsing rod of flesh to her mouth, sucking him, her tongue coiling about him while the tip of the intruder lodged in her throat.

Abruptly, Frost jerked himself from between her lips. Automatically Susan cupped her bosom, holding her bunched breasts up to him, expecting that he would stroke himself to a climax, jetting a stream of his semen over her. His jism would be the soothing unguent to calm the hurt in her tits. And Susan would glory in it, in being thus defiled.

Susan was mildly surprised, therefore, when Frost seemed to make no effort to finish with his hand the work begun by her lips and tongue. He merely cradled his swollen organ in the palm of his hand, directing it at the base of Susan's proffered breasts. As if in slow motion Susan saw the tiny pee-hole dilate. Only then did she realise, with a rush of heady sensual excitement, what exactly was about to happen.

An arc of golden urine burst from the tip of Frost's tenderly cradled penis to splash precisely over the plumply smooth surface of Susan's bunched bosom. It splashed up to wet her face, dampening her hair, crystal droplets dusting her shoulders. It cascaded along the channel between her tightly pressed breasts, trickled over the stiffly erect nipples, over her belly and her thighs. The golden shower seemed to last for hours as Frost played the torrent over his victim to soak her thoroughly.

Susan was almost delirious with joy. Here was true humiliation. Her senses were flooded with luxurious and erotic feelings of self-disgust. Little wonder then that, growing subtly at her core, a quiver of orgasm swept quietly over her just as Frost directed a final jet of urine between her parted lips.

"Hmm, I think we've both earned a little nap before dinner. You can clean this mess up later. I'll show you our bedroom now."

Joyfully Susan got to her feet, still dripping wet, and followed her temporary master up the stairs. Elliot had been right, as he invariably was. This change of scene was going to be ... painful, yes, certainly, but pleasurable too. Very pleasurable in ways that only a girl like Susan could appreciate.

## STREAKER

Jenny wriggled her bottom as she tried to get comfortable on the low pub stool. She crossed her legs and her black leather mini-skirt rode up to reveal another couple of inches of thigh. How she wished that John had not made her wear the wretched thing - it was more an exaggerated belt than a skirt anyway, hardly covering her bottom when she stood and almost leaving her bare from waist to ankle when she sat.

John had been careful, as well, to position her so that she sat, or rather perched, precariously, in full view of the drinkers at the bar. She was sure that she had already caught one particularly evil looking old man leering at her across the top of his glass while he enjoyed the sight of her well turned calves and honey golden tanned thighs. She just hoped that the blessed skirt didn't also let him glimpse her bare pubes beneath the inadequate pelmet of shiny leather.

She wiggled to place herself sideways on to her unwelcome admirer but this only resulted in the skirt hiking even higher so that the old lecher had a fine view of a portion of pale buttock flesh above the tanned skin of her shapely thigh.

John threaded his way through the sparse gathering of lunchtime drinkers, bearing glasses in both his hands. Carefully he set them down on the table against which Jenny was leaning in an attempt to steady herself on her perch. A broad grin broke through the bush of his curly beard.

"I see you're gathering an audience already." He nodded quite openly in the direction of the old man who continued unabashed to stare appreciatively at Jenny.

John sat down heavily and pushed a brimming glass of white wine towards Jenny then turned to the rat-faced man who, all this time, had sat silently watching Jenny's discomfort and awaiting his friend's return.

Jenny took a deep breath and mustered her courage. "John, I don't want to do this. Can't you just spank me like the last time? Please?" The last word came out thinly, lonely and imploring.

"Jenny, how many times must I tell you not to interrupt when I am in conversation. Black mark!" The tone was calm but with an edge, like a parent issuing a final warning to a misbehaving child. "Anyway, since you have interrupted me, am I to understand that you enjoyed the spanking I gave you?"

Jenny cringed inwardly at the memory and hastened to correct her husband's misapprehension.

"Oh no. No, not at all."

"That's as well since I may wish to spank you anyway after I've fetched you home from the police station."

The horrified look which, after a brief pause while she assimilated the enormity of the proposition, clouded Jenny's face, drew a boom of laughter from her husband and a complementary snigger from his weedy companion.

"Don't be so foolish. George here will be waiting in the car just on the other side of the bridge by the roundabout. You just run across the bridge, jump in the back seat and he'll whisk you off. Nothing to it. Now be quiet and drink your wine."

John settled back comfortably, sipped at his pint of dark amber beer and resumed his conversation with his male companion. Jenny, too, sipped her drink and listened distractedly to the two men as they discussed their plans for her when they had finished in the pub. For her own part she would have preferred to finish their drinks quickly and get on without more delay. This waiting just served to heighten the tension she was feeling and make the ordeal that awaited her seem all the more awful.

George, in the high pitched, whining voice that so aggravated her, had started to discuss the case of a girl who had streaked naked through the town centre, amazing Saturday shoppers, just a month or so before.

"... fine buxom girl too. Nice heavy tits like our dear Jenny's. Must have been a fine sight. But the best part," here a snigger, "the best part was that when the policeman caught up with her, his dog bit her on the bum."

Both men erupted in guffaws of hearty laughter.

At a superficially rational level Jenny realised that this was all simply intended to sport with her feelings. The worst of it was, deep down this ploy was having the desired effect. The prospect of what she must do in a few short minutes made her heart sink. She took another gulp of wine which made her feel a little better. John rarely allowed her alcohol and the effect of the wine on her senses was gratifyingly immediate. She felt the warm alcohol flush flood her cheeks and didn't feel quite so bad.

Some time later, after more light-hearted chaff calculated to depress their poor victim's spirits, John drained his glass and indicated that it was time to go. Buoyed up by the gentle cloud of alcohol fumes and a rush of adrenalin, Jenny didn't feel too apprehensive. At least the awful, humiliating experience would be over soon now that they were getting started.

This state of false confidence was soon dissipated, however, when Jenny saw her husband whisper confidentially into the ear of the old fellow who had persisted in eyeing her charms all of the while. The two men grinned at each other conspiratorially and, gathering up his grubby trenchcoat, the stranger followed Jenny and her two companions out into the afternoon sunshine.

As John lead her to the middle of the patch of neatly trimmed grass that stood at the centre of the market town, Jenny noted with some relief that on this early mid-summer afternoon there were not many people about to witness her embarrassment, just a few strolling couples and one or two avid window shoppers.

Standing in the middle of the town green Jenny could see the footpath stretching straight out before her, could see it rise over the hump of the little white stone bridge that spanned the river. The distance was hardly four hundred yards. To Jenny it might as well have been four miles.

"Now, count to twenty slowly so we have time to get to our positions, then off you go."

As John turned and began to walk away, Jenny started to count under her breath while her lips silently framed each word. Out of the corner of her eye she saw the old man take up his vantage point on a bench almost alongside her and fix his watery eyes on her as though anxious not to miss a moment of the promised spectacle. Jenny's nerves stretched taut. She turned away, trying to ignore him and hugged herself as she tried to control the shaking that was starting in her limbs.

A babble of chatter and a shriek of strident laughter as a group of people emerged from the pub drew Jenny's attention back in that direction. With a sickly weight in the pit of her stomach Jenny saw that they were just standing about and chatting on the pub forecourt. It seemed that the eyes of all of them were turned towards her. In fact, now the green seemed to be teeming with people and all of them were staring straight at her.

'... nineteen... twenty,' the mental count came to an end and it was time to start.

It didn't take many moments for Jenny to get ready as she was hardly wearing much to begin with. She tugged the loose, peasant blouse over her head, shucked the mini-skirt down her legs and kicked it, along with her shoes, to one side and there she was, stark naked, bare assed.

She sensed rather than saw the old man lean towards her and instinctively turned towards him. She stood for a long instant staring at him as he stared at her, running his eyes greedily over her plump and sweetly rounded bosom, over the swell of her hips and the rich copper of her pubic thatch.

With a gulp to fill her lungs she set off at a brisk pace, her bare feet slap, slap, slapping on the rough paving stones. The running was not the problem. John always made sure to include a few sprints in her weekly exercise programme and, besides, John's strict regime kept her fitter than most. It was being naked and having

217

all those eyes upon her, all watching the bounce of her heavy breasts against her ribcage, watching the jiggle of her fleshy buttocks and the flex and relax of thigh and calf.

She was sure that she could hear gasps and giggles from the onlookers as they realised that there was a naked person among them and they stood back to gawp.

She was on the bridge now. Tossing her head to clear a swirl of hair from her eyes, she caught sight of John at the crown of the bridge. She was aghast to see that he held a video camera and was pointing the lens right at her.

Now it felt like she was running through a sea of hot treacle as she imagined the events of the coming evening, replaying them in ghastly slow motion in her mind's eye. She saw herself draped naked over her husband's broad lap while the sole of his thick leather slipper thudded mercilessly against the cheeks of her squirming ass while before her on the television screen she would be forced to watch the shameful and humiliating events even now unfolding, again and again and again.

She crested the hump of the bridge, drawing level with her husband who waved cheerily from behind the camera. She shut her eyes, trying to ignore everything and spurted for the last few paces to the end of the bridge.

She slewed to a halt panting hard and glanced about her. With mounting panic she looked behind her then back down the road and over towards the far side of the roundabout. Where the hell was George? Where was the familiar rusty green saloon car?

In her panic she hardly noticed the man in shirt sleeves step towards her, was hardly aware of the blue serge jacket which he slipped about her shoulders.

"Just get into the back of the car please, Miss."

As she bent her head to enter she noticed the car was white and finally took in the broad red stripe that decorated its flank. Tears of helpless panic started in her eyes almost blinding her to the image of her portly husband and the skinny rodent by his side waving fondly from the far side of the road.

## PRACTICE! PRACTICE!

The spacious, high ceilinged room is brightly lit. The large windows, almost the full height of the room, give out onto a view of an extensive parkland where people stroll and an occasional horse-back rider passes. There are many such rooms in the civilised world. In New York the view would have been over Central Park, in Paris over the Bois de Boulogne, but here, in London, we are overlooking Hyde Park. Despite the headlong rush of the traffic outside no noise of the busy world penetrates to the room; all is deeply, forebodingly silent.

A young woman, hardly out of girlhood, sits with head bowed at a piano. It is a full size concert grand piano. She is formally dressed as if for a recital performance. A long black skirt reaching down to her feet covers her legs while a chaste, high necked, white blouse, a crisp ruffle at the front, completes her outfit. Her long chestnut hair, well brushed to shine in the intense light, frames a pretty, oval face which is marred only by the blemish of a distinct look of apprehension.

To all outward appearance there is no abnormality here - just a pretty and talented, albeit somewhat nervous, concert pianist at practice, preparing for her next engagement. The knowledgeable eye will, however, notice that her skirts are arranged after the fashion of Roissy, draped over the stool on which the young woman sits rather than gathered beneath her bottom. Indeed, after the fashion of Roissy, this demurely pretty creature wears no undergarments and the bare flesh of her

221

bottom is in direct contact with the cool, smooth leather of the piano stool.

Beside her, as she sits upright at the piano, her body held almost unnaturally stiffly erect, there stands a man. A man very obviously in late middle age. He stoops a little and his hair is streaked with grey. He is elegantly, yet austerely dressed.

The room is full of atmospheres. The air is distinctly chill despite the warm summer sunshine that filters through the tightly sealed window panes. This feeling of coldness is enhanced by the stark whiteness of the room's interior and by the virtual lack of any furnishing save the piano and a heavy leather armchair. Then, too, there is the almost palpable feeling of fear and apprehension that emanates from the young pianist. She is anxious to play well, anxious to please her master, but does she somehow doubt her capacity ever to fully please that demanding individual? Then again, there is the man: his frame barely containing the anger, the frustration and the malice that he feels by turns.

"Now, my dear," he begins, "for the Albert Hall concert I have decided that you shall have the privilege of playing my Piano Sonata Number 3. I trust that you appreciate that I am doing you a singular personal honour?"

"Thank you, Master Paul," she replies meekly, inclining her head in a token of acquiescence and, perhaps, gratitude.

"When I first performed this piece in Berlin in '70 it was rapturously received. I trust you have practiced sufficiently to enable you to do the piece justice."

"I have practiced as you directed, Master Paul." Now there was a slight tremor in the subdued voice.

"We shall see, shall we not? Let us begin with the first movement. And please try to remember that this is supposed to be a light, airy evocation of Spring and not a funeral dirge!"

The young woman, nerves already on edge, lays her hands over the keys and begins to play. At first all goes well. Then she plays a flat instead of a sharp, realises her mistake, loses her place in the score and all is confusion.

"Terrible, terrible! Start again, from the beginning. And this time, pay attention to the time signature!" he jets at her through clenched teeth.

She swallows hard and once again addresses the keyboard. This time she manages to get more than half-way into the first movement before Master Paul interrupts again. The tempo is all wrong. She must go back to the beginning and start again.

At last she manages to get through the whole of the first movement. Master Paul, his eyes shut, barely containing his disgust, turns to her and spits venomously,

"So, Janine, you claim to have worked on this piece?"

"Yes, Master Paul - for three weeks continuously."

"I think our ideas of what constitutes working at a piece differ radically! Your attempt on the first movement was execrable. There were some eighteen errors of interpretation when you finally got through the whole movement. Then there were elementary errors! Tell me, can you not read music? And for a pianist of your experience to play a simple sharp for a flat ... I am beyond words. You understand that I shall have to punish your laziness. My god! It was almost criminal."

Janine bites her lower lip and fixes her gaze on the keyboard. Past experience has taught her what is to happen next. When she speaks her voice is a timorous quiver, a virtual whisper,

"I am sorry, Master Paul. Yes, please punish me for my laziness."

"Very well. Take off your skirt and kneel up on the chair over there," Master Paul commands sharply, indicating the only other piece of furniture in the room.

Janine rises and fumbles with the fastenings of the long black skirt. It is soon in a heap about her feet. As we have remarked, she wears no undergarments and the pale rondure of her buttocks is now displayed. Stepping out of the skirt which has pooled about her feet, she walks slowly, head bowed, over to the armchair and kneels on the seat as directed, parting her legs slightly, pushing her buttocks out, using her arms to support her weight against the chair back. This is a familiar posture to her and she needs no instruction - this she has already practiced to perfection.

Master Paul stands behind her and slaps upward at her exposed bum-cheek, his lightly cupped hand connecting - thwaak - with the fleshy lower lobe. Janine's bumflesh ripples under the impact and Janine utters a little, surprised cry, "Owch!"

"Yes, that's right, my girl. Since you cannot play the piano for me, let me hear you sing," he remarks bitterly.

Steadily, Master Paul spanks the girl's out thrust bottom, reddening the pale lobes as she squeals, "Owch" and "Oww, my bottom!" The fleshy globes jiggle under the assault of his hand until, after some eighteen slaps, he desists.

"Now, young lady, take your seat and let us see what you can do with - or should I say to - the second movement."

Naked from the waist down, Janine returns to the piano, on her way affording Master Paul a delightful glimpse of the chestnut thatch that covers her Mount. She again takes her seat, sighing as the caress of the leather seat cools her hotly stinging buttocks.

"Now, pay attention to the tempo. And please read the time signature, that is what it is there for. So, begin!"

Her lip trembling, hosts of butterflies in violent flight in her tummy, Janine again lays her hands on the keys and begins to play. Her confidence is not enhanced by knowing that Master Paul has an excellent view of her bare legs and backside as she plays. Of course, the inevitable results of nervousness obtrude and, if anything, her attempt on the second movement is far worse than her performance with the first.

Master Paul lets his young protege continue for perhaps five minutes before he finds himself unable to contain his impatience for a moment longer. He bangs a fist on the keyboard, setting off a discordant jangle of notes.

"Stop! Stop! Stop! You are desecrating my music. This is terrible. Such discord! That last bar should have been - ta, ta, ta-ta, tarom, ta,ta," and he beats out the phrasing on the lid of the piano. "Now begin again!"

It is as much as poor oppressed Janine can do to contain the trembling in her hands. Her stomach feels empty. The stinging in her buttocks from the spanking has subsided to a dull ache but even this is forgotten in her fearfulness, in her agitation. Again she addresses the keyboard. Her eyes are starting to water and she cannot read the music in front of her through the blur of hot, salty tears. She begins again.

The result is disastrous. Master Paul is virtually squirming with disgust. His toes tap imperiously as Janine assaults (that is the only word for it) his cherished piece of music. At last she manages to get to the end of the second movement and sits, wriggling in discomfort on the piano stool, awaiting the Master's verdict.

"Stand up please!" Master Paul demands sharply. "Stand up and face me. Look me in the eyes!"

Janine, conscious of her bare limbs and her naked belly beneath the chaste white blouse, stands trembling, looking into the enraged gaze of Master Paul. She clasps her hands behind her, resting on the swelling outcurve of her bare bum. Already, hopeless tears are again welling up in her eyes and start to trickle down her pale cheeks.

"So you tell me you have practiced. That was atrocious - an insult. Even the worst schoolboy could have made a better attempt. I give you my finest, my proudest work and you rape it - nothing less!"

"But ... but ... Master Paul," Janine begins dissolving into floods of tears. Her face screws up and bitter salt tears make tracks of translucent silver down her blushing cheeks. "Oh, you make me so nervous, so on edge!"

"So, you wont be nervous before an audience? Come now, it is only your laziness and your culpable inattention that you must blame."

Janine hangs her head in shame as Master Paul enumerates at length and corrects the multitude of errors she has made in the second movement of his precious sonata. This is not a new experience; it has in fact been daily ritual in the three years since first she became Master Paul's pupil. Now, before her looms the third, the final and the infinitely more taxing last movement. But first:

"I think you need a little more encouragement before you assault the third movement," Master Paul remarks. "Janine, take off the rest of your clothes."

Automatically, obediently, Janine's fingers are busy with the buttons of the white cotton blouse. She shrugs it from her shoulders and reaches behind to unclasp her bra. Then she is naked, her firm young breasts openly on display, her belly, her flaring hips, everything. Although the scene has often been played before she is still embarrassed to be naked before Master Paul. Her cheeks flush and she crosses her arms over her breasts, vainly covering the nipples which are already puckered by the cold. Her head hangs in shame.

"No false modesty, my girl," remarks Master Paul as he picks up a leather strap from where it has lain all this time on the piano. "Kneel on the chair."

Janine uncovers her breasts and walks to the chair, maybe a little hesitantly, and kneels again on the seat, her legs slightly parted as before, her trunk bent forward and her bottom pushed out to receive the new dose of punishment.

'Whaaak!' Master Paul smashes the leather strap right over the plumpest cushion of bumflesh. Janine throws back her head, lips drawn back in a rictus grin of pain and howls, wolflike in the still air. A bright red mark forms across the middle of her pale bottom. Steadily Master Paul lays on with the strap allowing his victim to savour each blow as a separate and distinct torment. Blows slap over the whole semiglobe of pale and quaking flesh, even reaching down as far as her upper thighs, quivering the ripe flesh of her fesses.

Then the tears really begin to flow. Deep sobs wrack the young girl's slender frame as her body shudders under the blows.

"Now do you feel ashamed? Do you feel punished as you deserve?" demands Master Paul between strokes.

"Oh yes, yes ... yess! Yes Master!" declares Janine between sobs, her small but so shapely breasts shuddering.

"Well, learn your lesson well," and another stroke of the strap quivers her bottom which is now held relaxed and offering no resistance to the angry onslaught.

"P-p-please, no more," blubbers Janine, her eyes stinging with the salty tears.

Master Paul slaps her again - once, twice - as she jerks her body, squirming to avoid the strap. "Now stand up," he commands. Janine faces him, cuffing the tears from her eyes. He hands her a handkerchief, strokes her hair, rearranges a few stray strands from out of her eyes.

"Alright, you may sit down. Control yourself and let us see what you make of the third movement. Read the tempo and remember the crescendo at bars twenty to twenty-five." His tone is business-like but no longer threatening.

Naked, the sobs jouncing her firm, tight breasts delightfully, Janine sits at the piano. This time the cool leather affords but scant relief to her poor punished bottom. Her bumcheeks glow hotly and the stinging is intense. Somehow, though, she has to pull herself together and do justice to the music. She must, she will.

Suddenly, as if for the first time, she becomes intensely aware of her nudity. There she is, stark naked and sitting at a grand piano before an uncurtained window. She has a clear and uninterrupted view of the park. What then can the passers by in the park see of her? She flushes hotly, the butterflies in her tummy again take flight while her hands and knees begin to tremble.

Her worries are needless. The window on the second floor of the large house stares blankly down on the park. Nobody can see a thing and in fact nobody casts so much as a second glance up towards the window.

"Go on, play!" insists Master Paul.

Janine takes a deep breath and addresses herself to the task in hand. She is, however, still acutely conscious of her nudity. The pain in her bottom is really intense - the fire that Master Paul has kindled simply will not abate. Again he is sighing and tapping his foot. Janine can barely concentrate on the music.

Her performance of this third movement is, if it were possible, worse than her attempts on the two preceding movements. The tempo is wrong and whole bars of the music are transposed to make a nonsense of the melody. Twice Master Paul stops her and with a terse comment makes her return to the beginning where she must start all over again. By the time when, mercifully, the end has been reached, Janine is again in tears, this time in frustration at her inability to compose herself and ignore the virtually continuous litany of complaint and criticism that flows from her mentor.

"Again, I ask you," begins master Paul, looking skyward, "if you believe you have practiced hard enough? Bad enough that you seem unable to keep time but you are wholly unfamiliar with the piece. Let me remind you that there are just three weeks to go before you perform this work before an audience. An audience, I might add, who will prove much more critical than I."

Poor Janine feels herself very naked, very alone and very cold. She hugs herself, clasping her arms around her bosom, bending her head low over the keyboard, her attractive face contorted with crying, her body heaving with heart deep sobs.

"It seems to me that you need one final lesson before we break off today," begins Master Paul. "I really think that I am altogether too soft with you. Your approach to my piece was ruinous, simply ruinous. I shall expect better of you tomorrow and I think you need a caning to remind you of your duty. Now, climb up on the piano stool and get yourself ready."

Janine, without another word, closes the lid of the piano and assumes a kneeling position on the piano stool. She bends over and places her hands on the lid of the instrument making her bottom stick out pertly as she had been bidden.

Her poor fesses still sting from the strapping she received not forty minutes before and now she has to endure the cane. But there can be no escape, no remission. She bites her lip and tries to control her sobbing.

"I think a dozen strokes will serve our purpose quite adequately. Do you agree?"

Agree or not, Janine will have to endure them, perched naked, conical breasts hanging succulently beneath her.

"Yes, Master Paul. You are very kind to take so much trouble with me."

Janine hears the 'Swiiish' of the cane as it cleaves the air behind her. Then searing pain invests her bottom as the well aimed blow connects with the meaty globes with a force that almost jerks her from her perch. Involuntarily she screams. Dimly, behind her, she hears Master Paul intoning the count of her punishment, "One ... two ... how does that feel, my dear?"

"Oh, oh, agony ... my bum is on fire. P-pl-please no!"

"Five ... six ..."

And thus the punishment continues. The ache already within her from the spanking and the strap is now eclipsed by the fiery strokes of the cane. Master Paul plies the rod over her flinching buttocks and thighs, even striking at the backs of her knees in a controlled frenzy. Janine squeals and finds she can cry no more - the well of her tears has quite dried up.

"Eleven ... twelve!" At last it is over. For Janine nothing exists but the hot stinging in her buttocks and her thighs.

For a few moments Master Paul lets her remain as she is. A sardonic smile of satisfaction lights his dour face as he surveys the bright crimson stripes he has raised on poor Janine's youthful flesh. They stand stark and angry against the mellow pink blush that colours her flesh from the earlier mistreatment with palm and leather.

"Now stand up and face me."

Her face still twisted in a grimace of pain, Janine stands, her legs atremble and threatening to give out on her at any moment, and as steadily as she is able looks her tormentor in the eye. Gingerly her hands creep behind her in a reflex attempt to comfort her sore and burning nates.

"There remain three hours before dinner. Use some of that time to practice diligently before you come to me."

"Thank you Master Paul," Janine whispers, "I promise you I will try harder."

Satisfied for the moment, Master Paul has already turned on his heel and left the room, leaving the trembling girl to recover herself as best as she can. He has hardly stepped ten paces before, once again, the strains of his music fill the air.

Janine finishes the piece once more. Without the distraction of Master Paul's glowering presence it has gone quite well. She is calmer and quietly pleased with herself. Just the dull ache in her bottom and the more insistent urging aroused in her sex are left to remind her of her humiliation at the hands of her unremitting taskmaster.

Well schooled, trained to an exacting level of obedience, Janine knows precisely what must happen now. With some eagerness she leaves the piano and, bare feet slip-slapping on the polished wooden floor, makes her way along a corridor to a room on the other side of the apartment.

A heavy curtain has been drawn across the window to block out the brilliant sunlight and the bedroom is bathed in a twilight gloom. Master Paul, lying supine on the bed, a black silk sheet draped across his naked loins, sees Janine through half-lidded eyes as a pale and ghostlike form in the dusk.

Nervously she enquires: "Was that better?"

"Yes, much improved - with hard work it might become acceptable." High praise and highly valued coming from such a renowned perfectionist.

"Thank you, Master Paul." Her voice is sweet and soft. "May I pleasure you now?"

A curt nod of the head grants permission. A soft hand reaches out to lightly stroke and then tangle the grizzled mat of hair adorning Master Paul's broad chest. A sharp finger nail scratches gently over a male nipple teasing it to erection before her hand sweeps languidly down his torso to brush the carelessly arranged sheet from his body.

His penis lies thick and heavy across his lower abdomen. Gently, Janine curls her fingers around the thick, living tube of flesh.

There is no need for further foreplay. The music and the strap have performed the function of arousal sufficiently for both of them. Master Paul's manhood is swollen and hard, twitching importunately under

Janine's slender fingers. She feels quite distinctly the hot pulse of blood in the great vein. Her own sex is liquid desire, musk oozing between hypersensitive nether lips.

In an easy, sinuous movement she straddles his body, fitting the head of his penis into the welcoming socket of her womanhood. With an animal groan of pleasure she feeds him into herself until the welcome intruder is fully embedded within. He is massively thick, the hard flesh forcing apart the supple muscles of her fleshy sheath, forcing her to accommodate its mass.

With a sigh of absolute bliss she settles upon the rod of flesh, feeling him twitch and move inside her, tasting the sensation of fullness, of swelling maleness trapped inside her sex.

Janine places her palms against the flat, muscular chest of her master, lightly supporting herself as she crouches over him, her small conical breasts swinging gently from side to side. She holds herself motionless while the youthfully resilient muscles of her sex work against the rigid pole of living flesh buried within her core. Each ripple of her supple muscles along the length of his thick manhood draws a sigh of pleasure and approbation from the lips of Master Paul as he luxuriates under the ministrations of her body.

With a final sigh Master Paul raises his torso from the bed and grasps Janine firmly about the hips. His fingers digging firmly into the pliant flesh signal that she should move on to the final movement of their sexual symphony.

Working against his firm grasp Janine raises herself to let the rigid python that has speared her belly emerge from her pitch dark cavern, gleaming slickly, coated with her juices. Slowly, luxuriously, her eyes closed in a sexual ecstasy, she lowers herself back over the meaty rod, twisting herself in a corkscrew motion to draw a deep groan of enjoyment from Master Paul's lips. She raises herself again, almost letting the thick man meat slip from between her nether lips before again lowering herself to lodge the beast within her drooling sex.

Master Paul's grip tightens, firm fingers pinching ivory flesh to raise red weals, urging her on to their mutual crescendo. Obediently, Janine quickens the pace, riding up and down on the fat pole of flesh, gasping with her own pleasure, her head tossing in manic abandon. Suddenly, with a deep throated groan, Master Paul is coming inside her, semen jetting from his throbbing manhood to lave her womb as his teeth clamp viciously over the crown of a trembling, girlish breast.

Janine squeals but the cry of pain has barely left her lips before her body shudders and she groans in her own climax.

Slumped against her master's unyielding breast, Janine is allowed but a few moments to recover her senses before a curt command sends her off to prepare herself for dinner.

Still lying on his back in the half-darkness, Master Paul allows himself the last satisfaction of reviewing in his mind's eye the events of that afternoon. For the thousandth time he congratulates himself on having noticed his young charge's submissive streak.

The merest trace of a smile grows over his lips. The child is really developing quite well. Her performance this afternoon had been quite creditable - indeed, quite creditable. But it would never do to risk breeding over confidence by lavishing fulsome praise at such an early stage. No, on the contrary, he must goad her, drive her hard. And she must practice! Practice until her fingers ache. Practice while her sore bottom smarts. Practice!

*This is how the first Silver Moon book (Erica:Property of Rex) opened:*

Paint was peeling from the woodwork of the dingy inner-city terrace house at the end of the pathetic strip of unkempt garden. The family might well have gone away after all that publicity: neighbours get very militant when youngsters are abused, even in this foulest of London slums.

The front door was ajar. I thought I heard crying from inside, or perhaps this was an abandoned kitten. Nobody answered my knock. The noise that had disturbed me stopped abruptly, that was all.

I pushed open the creaking door. It led to a bare narrow uncarpeted passage. In front I could see into a cheerless kitchen with unwashed dishes piled high in a sink with a dripping tap. A door was half open on my left. I went in, and there she was, lying naked on her stomach on a shabby green couch.

She turned over and sat up in alarm, an extremely pretty girl, obviously the one I was seeking, the one mentioned in those titillating press reports I had brooded over all this time. She tried to cover herself with the only protection she had, a very small cushion. For a moment big bewildered blue eyes peeped through long reddish-auburn hair which hung over her face in a haze, then she jumped to her feet and scampered to a corner as far away from me as she could get, turning to face me shyly, shaking her head so that the hair swung behind her. She was holding the cushion to her loins, but it could not conceal the fact that she had a perfect little figure, slim but nicely rounded. She stood very erect, which drew attention to those budding breasts, so high and firm.

There was no heating or comfort in that bare room, apparently no one else in the house.

"Are you Erica?" I asked.

"Yes." It was almost a whisper. She was shrinking into the corner. She had the wide sort of mouth that so easily shows the upper teeth, and hers were good, regular and very white.

"Where's your step-Mother?"

"G-gone to the pub."

"Does she always leave you like this, no clothes?"

"Oh no, but I mustn't go out because -"

"Because what?"

"Because, well you see, Uncle Willie is coming to - to punish me."

That troubled me, of course. In fact I had been troubled about 'Erica' ever since that first newspaper story - I have changed all names, for obvious reasons. As she cowered in the corner my eyes dwelt on her skin, so very smooth, a beautiful light brown, maybe olive, verging on golden, inviting the fingers to slide over it, all over it, to explore its shyness and secret recesses ...

I licked my lips. "I think I'll wait for your step-mother. Will she be long?"

"They'll be back any minute!"

"And your Uncle Willie is coming to punish you?" It seemed incredible. "What do you mean, punish?"

She hesitated, biting her full lower lip. "He - he'll beat me, I think. With the belt, I expect, the leather one that hangs by my bed."

THE DARKER SIDE is the third book in the SILVER MINK series of erotic fiction for women - which, we have to admit, are mostly sold to men!

SILVER MINK books present the same type of storyline - dominant men and submissive women - as are to be found in the Silver Moon titles, but do so a more subtle way and with more emphasis on romance: a little more up-market, perhaps!

They are available from Silver Moon Reader Services on the same arrangements as Silver Moon titles, see overleaf.

ISBN 1-897809-09-3 WHEN THE MASTER SPEAKS (Josephine Scott)

In 1869 Clarisse runs away from her country home, and excessive parental discipline, to the delights of London, where she finds discipline can have a deeper and more pleasurable meaning than she ever realised.

In 1969 Lauren leaves the country - and a broken relationship - for those same delights, where she also finds that love can have painful yet pleasurable overtones.

In a house in Fleet Street past and present blend into a fascinating tapestry of pain and pleasure.

ISBN 1-897809-13-1 AMELIA, Josephine Oliver.

A Tale of Punishment and Retribution.

Amelia falls under the sway of a 'Country Gentleman' whose attitude towards women was learned among the slave owners of an American Plantation of the 1850s.

He submits here to deeper and deeper discipline and degradation, until at last the tables are turned.

And, as Mistress, Amelia knows exactly how to exercise her new won powers.

*Free extracts from these novels are avilable on request whilst stocks last. A free 16 page booklet of extracts from current Silver Moon and Silver Mink titles is also available, and free monthly updates are sent to those on our mailing list.*